Water Log

Hugo Clemente

Translated from the Spanish by
Peter Kahn

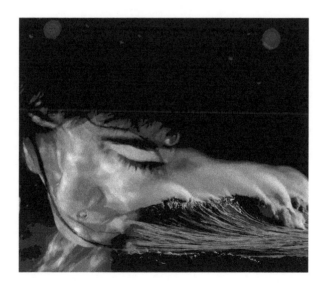

SPUYTEN DUYVIL
New York City

Thanks to all the music that powerfull and premeditadely inspired *Water Log*. Songs that spalshed the text either shaped as notes or lyrics: La perrera, Rapsusklei, Fabio McNamara, The Beastie Boys, Commando 9mm, The Ramones, Veruca Salt, Atari Teenage Riot, Family, Toots and The Maytals, Lars Fredericksen and the Bastards, LPR, The Mighty Roars, José Luís Moreno Ruíz, Shotta, Gil Scott-Heron, Mötorhead, Narco, Rosendo, Sólo los Solo, Siniestro Total, The Street Walking Cheetahs, Electric Six, El Gran Puzzle Cózmico, Iggy and the Stooges, Turbonegro, Supersuckers, Batiscafo, Trevor Truble, Whitey, The Nomads, Jimmy Smith, Fats Walker, Lutoslavski, Jelly Roll Morton, Susana Rinaldi, Cake, Nofx, The Accidents, The Kings of Nuthin´, El Robe, Javier Corcobado, Chet Baker, The Mad Capsule Market, Dead Kennedys, Camarón de la Isla, Howie B, Enrique Morente & Lagartija Nick, The Music, Gonzales, The 5,6,7,8´s, Los Enemigos, Richard Cheese, Snuff, The International Noise Conspiracy, The Jon Spencer Blues Explosion, Zeke, The Pinkertones, Los Granadians del Espacio Exterior, Pixies, Booker T & The Mg´s, Lords of Altamont, Geno Washington, Alton Ellis, 713avo Amor, The Queers, The Toasters, Guttermouth, Rocky Erickson, Pánico, New Bomb Turks, Parálisis Permanente, Air, Gallon Drunk, Lalo Schifrin, The Lazy Cowgirls, Les Thugs, Peaches, Propagandhi, Reverend Horton Heat, El Vez, Señor No, Herbie Hancock, Cal Tjader and Woody Carr &The El Caminos.
I´m sure I am missing more than one.
And thanks to all the people who inspired, supported and collaborated.
Thanks Pibita.

©2018 Hugo Clemente
translation © 2018 Peter Kahn
ISBN 978-1-947980-38-9
Cover art & Design: Luís González Cruz www.apolinart.com
Authors Pic: Toni Rodriguez www.tonyshoots.com

Library of Congress Cataloging-in-Publication Data

Names: Clemente, Hugo, 1973- author. | Kahn, Peter, 1958- translator.
Title: Water log / Hugo Clemente ; translated from the Spanish by Peter Kahn.
Other titles: Cuaderno de agua. English
Description: New York : Spuyten Duyvil, 2018.
Identifiers: LCCN 2018002272 | ISBN 9781947980389
Classification: LCC PQ6703.L3825 C8313 2018 | DDC 863/.7--dc23
LC record available at https://lccn.loc.gov/2018002272

For Concha, the godmother

Zero
Man Overboard!

To seduce you, confuse you, almost deceive you, leave you stranded in the current. The moment you come below, your iceberg cracks, the light at the end of the tunnel is no freight train. I can feel the sheen of your iceberg, everything's cool, I'm in place, in the moment. It'll be here and now. I can shout that it'll be me who comes out on top. I change my position, kneeling as I remove your clothes, sliding the fabric from your skin, as it gently resists and clings. Vertical vertigo, tension on the wall as I find your petite breast, beautiful and firm in its convictions. And I recognize your navel, its perpendicular consistency. I reach the peak when I can no longer breathe and all begins to collapse. The curves, the movement, the trembling, the liquid bursts. Then, after the roar, all is silence. You go slack and I fall to pieces.

ONE
GRAY

The ocean was gray. A truly black and arrogant sky, preparing to rage down on us. Its reflection looming over a restless sea, its discharge brewing. A cloudburst aiming lead at us as we meekly raise our hands. In the end, we have to flee the beach, get home and lower the blinds.

Two
Really Screwed

Of all the concessions to inertia in your life, the worst is cleaning your work shoes. It makes no sense, except to have momentarily brilliant footwear. We should distrust all kinds of dry-cleaning. It's the worst of the lies we've been force-fed. To make our beds, only to systematically unmake them every night is stupid, although there is something soothing about sliding into freshly stretched sheets. As you wait for them to warm up, time seems to pass at a different speed. Shining your shoes with black shoe polish reeking of petroleum, every two or three nights, adds nothing, it only self-perpetuates. You could do it every twelve hours, but then you would cross some line that separates professional responsibility from mental disorder. If obsession and compulsion, hand in hand, come to visit you, you might seem to be a total genius, a meticulous serial killer, or the best tool for whoever can find a use for you. To shine what will inevitably get dirty again as it drags over the ground only demonstrates that we have been convinced by some malicious sleight of hand that we can somehow reject our condition as plantigrades, web-footed creatures, as inhabitants of a planet that covers us with dust. When you accept such a truth, they've really got you screwed.

THREE
ANVIL

I don't know why, but sometimes, when I kiss you, you taste like metal. It happens all of a sudden. You have it hidden in your mouth. I suck on your lips, trying to extract the pulp. They're massive and alive. Swollen and clumsy as they wander over my face. My mouth, your base camp. We nip at each other's lips and sometimes tongues. We bite gingerly, searching. When we find the other, with a little bit of flesh between the teeth, we try to devour. We spend long stretches of time in this way, trading saliva back and forth, negotiating. All of a sudden your upper lip has a stainless steel taste, like paper clips and batteries. It drives me crazy all over again. It's strong and sharp, like nails. I look for it everywhere in your mouth and on your lower lip, which has a red aftertaste. Poisoned, I search everywhere my tongue can reach. You release nine thousand pins, perforating my veins. Yet I search for the metal all through your body, your neck, and I come back to your mouth. Your eyes are closed. It's always like this. You don't realize you've swallowed an anvil. You don't care. The taste spreads through your body, lost for a while in your throat, until another day, when I simply kiss you and the concentrated juice of knives and safety pins sprays into my mouth all over again. All those rusty pins, striking me in the bull's eye, second after second, sinking my heart.

FOUR
H$_{TWO}$O

It's an element, but of what gender? Water is masculine, *el agua*, according to the article that precedes it, even though it's unstable and slippery like a capricious female. The sea is bisexual. *El mar*, we all say. *La mar*, say the salty dogs. Difficult to define, to contain, to obtain, and to recognize, because it adopts the most unexpected forms. An enormous lip, so irresistible you can't stop paddling until you've tried to kiss it, an infinite liquid coffin, a dump, a horizon, a postcard. A drenched angel, a turquoise demon, a storyteller, a perpetual percussion beat, seven pairs of love songs. A deep sea monster crashing upon itself, over and over. And who doesn't know its formula? H$_2$0, glaring in blue and pink neon, crowning the fashionable terrace below a hotel on Summertime Beach. Everything is water or its absence. You and I are more than half water. Seventy percent, they say. I'd like to know if this is still true at an altitude of four thousand two hundred meters, or on Sundays at noon. It cures everything, and it also carries everything away. Life and oxide. It can resuscitate you, or take you by the hand to your death, and it always looks the same, colorless, insipid, and transparent. I try to connect with it, throwing my Log at it from every beach, trying to land it on top of a wave and waiting for the tide to return it to me soaked. In my Log I find garbage and wreckage, flora and coral, fish, legends, petroleum and the drowned. Salt, waves, seaweed, and sand. It slips through my fingers, surges, and drenches everything.

Five
Dogs

For Stevenson, surfers are like dogs. According to Stevenson, anyone who spends more than twenty minutes playing in the water, and doesn't drown or sink, is a surfer. Like dogs because they won't let go of the wave once they've sunk their teeth into it, like a dog with a bone that falls from the master's table. He calls them rabid when there are lots of dogs but few waves. He swears that he has seen more than one lift his leg to mark his territory. Territoriality quickly dissipates in the ocean, he says. He doesn't know what he's talking about. Rigid bloodhounds, with bent legs, frozen, as they signal with their snouts a likely prey on the horizon. But most importantly, Stevenson thinks surfers are like those irritating dogs that keep coming back with the stick, again and again, so their owner has to throw it, celebrating with peals of piercing barks. It makes no difference how often you throw the stick to the surfers, they'll always come back with the stick in their mouths, nervously wagging their tails, twisting their bodies as they run from one side to another, waiting for The Hand to do its thing. "They're like retrievers in the water," says Stevenson, brushing the curls of hair back from his face, waiting to be able to put them in a ponytail. "Then they become even more like dogs, in the streets of some town, beneath the scorching August sun." He dries the sweat from his forehead with the back of his hand and can't help but look at it. He's sweating like a pig. "Lying around on the corners, practically dead, trying to find some shade."

They wander around on the beaches in swimsuits, flip-flops and hoods with visors. They park their vans and take out their boards. They smoke and chat, giving high-fives or fist bumps. A few, sometimes, go into the water. Some are content with posing, leafing through the monthly surf magazines. Stevenson isn't one of those who likes to be confused with a dog.

Six
Security

I was running late. The fault, once again, was the ocean's. You warned me. I responded by trying to give you a kiss on your full lips, but you turned and I only managed to graze your cheek, still smelling of sleep. I smiled as I pulled the boards out of the van. The northwest swell was surging a meter and a half—that is, a meter and a half in the islands. Here they measure the wave from the back side, they calculate the height of the hump, but then the wall measures twice that. The summer was ripe, dry and shriveled. So much power was not to be wasted, right in the middle of the pitiful vision of an oil barge on the horizon for days, when the beaches in the morning were covered with portable refrigerators, shrieks and bouncing balls. I shaved, pulled my work shoes on without untying the laces, by dint of force. I tucked in my shirt. I noticed my hair was stiff from the saltwater. I was arriving late but happy, with limber body and my mind resting at the gentle gray end of the scale. I left the house running, shouting see you later as I ran out the door. You shook my head, knowing you were right. I started the car and sighed with pleasure. I tried to put on my necktie as I drove to the airport. I don't know who I was trying to kid. At Topsy-Turvy International, I ran from the revolving doors to the area for domestic flights. They still hadn't called me from the office. Maybe I'd manage to get there during those minutes of grace conceded to me by the shift manager. I reached the security gate and a water bubble sweetly popped in my temples. I smiled at the security check line without anyone paying me mind.

The palm of a hand stopped me just as I was about to go through the arches of a metal detector. A firm hand, not very big, buttressed by an outstretched arm, connected to a uniformed body on which rested a face at whose center a crooked nose arrogantly sucked up mucous.

"You can't go through here."

I raised my eyes and met another pair of eyes, looking right through me and beyond, but somehow familiar. It was a man with black pants tucked inside his storm trooper boots and a thick gold chain, and here I was with my tie and accoutrements. We both seemed out of place.

"You're not supposed to go through here. It's a new regulation."

"But I have my identification card." (How do I know this guy?)

He shook his head like a plastic bobble-head dog in the back window of a car.

He spoke as if we were in the doorway to Pachá, the nightclub, and I was wearing white socks. I saw him recently.

"What do you think, you're in a fucking club? Or what?" I stepped forward.

Now there seemed to be something like steam coming out from his nose.

The smoke that angry bulls snort in the cartoons. His nose had been split, obviously, by someone with less patience than me. A large nose, a Marian apparition in a forest, glowing against the aura of golden hair.

We were grappling with each other when another member of the airport security team, with more authority than the blond, intervened to restore some order.

"What's going on here?" The question emerged from under a well-groomed moustache.

"Nothing. Except this guy seems to think we're at the entrance to a disco."

I had to explain myself better as I was forgetting they were law enforcement agents. The one with the broken honker took a step to the side, pretending acquiescence, muttering something under his breath to provoke me into challenging him, What did you say? and we would come back together like two rutting rams, butting horns, while his superior explained that the rules had changed and that the guy was new, so I should try to understand. I did.

"Shit! This is how you train new people?"

I was in a rush so I pushed past them, figuratively hissing and more literally passing through the arches of the metal detector, without showing any identification at all. They were nervous and didn't pay any attention to these details. As I walked away I made a show of staring at the blond with the crooked beak, smiling at him.

"Now I know where I know you from. You were on the beach this morning." His eyes sparkled as he bit his lip and hooked his thumbs through his regulation ammunition belt, hitching up his pants.

"Nice waves, huh?"

I could hear them cursing my mother as I turned away, whistling a song by La Perrera.

SEVEN
TIC TOC

Two needles on a watch pointing at my head with the precision of a plastic surgeon's scalpel. They're on the verge, on the dot, of dumping their load of unfinished chores on me, postponed obligations, blockages, and I'll see if tomorrow I can square things away. The sand and the sun were the first to fetter us in Time. The wind erases tracks on the dunes, the remains of a wound that never quite heals, now transformed into diminutive but heavy ballast rocks to be carried home. It all sticks to the skin like a crust. And then there's the tic-toc which we learned for sleeping and waking, diluted by the murmur of the waves and, somewhere inside, the memory is established of our last date with urgency. Now we are pursued by fake watches that hardly fit on the peddlers' wrists. Travelers to Indonesia are asked to bring them back or, even better, trips are organized to China with empty suitcases. They return packed full of imitation rolexes, breitlings, and ralph laurens. If you ask them about the Great Wall, they'll tell you they saw it from the airplane, between sips from beverages they were given free of charge. If you ask them about the Chinese food they'll tell you about revulsion, of stewed dogs and, finally, they'll smile, having arrived safe and sound at home, as if amazed at the fact that a big mac tastes the same everywhere. Even if you don't ask them, they'll tell you that in Bangkok they were very fortunate, that with a hundred euros they had more than enough to drink through the night with one of those delightful creatures of the night who happily accompanied them to their room for some heavy breathing. Although you've heard enough, they'll go on to add that they're gorgeous and irresistible. They've tried to give me two of those low-budget tributes to opulence, and I've had to argue my way out both times. It's not a watch but rather a chronograph, they say, offended. I would never be proud of spending more than ten thousand dollars on a watch, I'd never feel fulfilled wearing one of those, and I would never feel smart saying that I only paid two hundred dollars for one that only a self-considered expert could detect as being different, even though, by its appearance, it doesn't look submersible.

Eight
Bermuda

Three of us were still in the water, the rest were drying off in their vans. Some had spread out over the beach to show their faces and thereby justify parading their seventy-euro T-shirts through their neighborhoods, no such luck for some of the others. It was a nasty day, the water cold, a marble sky. A strong current and waves breaking like deadbolts. You could only tell the good ones by getting on top of them. I figured I'd been in the water for about two hours. Out of two hours, how much time had I spent upright on my board? Three minutes? Three out of one hundred twenty? It's disagreeable to paddle and swallow water, to avoid sets, dodge surfers, slide over rocks when you get into the water, deal with the cold in winter, the sand in your seams, to leave the house in the dark of the morning to catch the waves just right. Only when you're out on the ocean, waiting for a set, does it all make sense. Cutting the wave with my fins, silencing the roar of the water. It's like falling in love with someone who pretends you don't exist. Your friends suggest you forget her, and you know they're right. Meanwhile, you inhale your love deeply because you know it will never happen. I relinquished a wave to a kid who looked at me, perplexed, and he also let it go. After that he relaxed. His furrowed brow went smooth, and perhaps his lats too , and when we both ended up on another peak he spoke to me, kind of sideways, on account of what the other locals might say. I continued against the sea, taking a few unwelcome swallows. I caught a few and, when I was leaving, I looked up at the cliffs. The land seemed to be trying to tell me something, but the murmur of the sea was still too loud—go home, get out of here. I crossed paths with the kid again, who politely said goodbye. The vans had long disappeared from the boardwalk. I smiled as I waited for the last wave, the one that would take me to the shore. Wondering. Why would someone put on cologne to go swimming? As I was drying off, another question came to me, with much more urgency. Something that had been bothering me since I arrived on The Island. Something you could see in the north and the south: the things they wore with the same unabashed pride, uncertainty, and indifference, the scum, the shubies, the ocean divas, the hipsters and even the hard-core gringos. In a way that is incomprehensible, in the eyes of reason, every one of them goes swimming with shorts on under their swim shorts, which around here they call Bermudas. But why? Hawaiian flowers over black briefs. What for? Then, when they're through swimming, they take off the shorts and the swim suits. They dry off and put on underwear and shorts, and then, sometimes, they put on another pair of swim shorts! There must be an explanation for all this. It could be the same legend that justifies that little girls of nine years old play with buckets and shovels, building sandcastles, wearing string bikinis. Such abominable swimwear to dress such happy little creatures, unaware of the twisted universe of adults. Madame, please, behave yourself for the love of God and let your little girl play nude on the beach. The top part of the bikini is unnecessary on your little girl, she doesn't even have breasts yet. And the poor dear spends more time trying to get that strand of dental floss out of her butt than filling her pail with sand. Fortunately, she is still unaware of flirtation or what it implies. Oh, and the underpants just go too far for your little boy.

Nine
Dressed in White

Feli was dressed all in white the night of San Juan. The sleeveless T-shirt contrasted his freshly tanned shoulders. Thai fisherman pants; right down to the sandals, it was a complete outfit. White is not worn well by those who want to, but only by those who can. The beach was thick with revelers, bonfires, and the aroma of sardines roasting on improvised grills in the sand. The night of San Juan in Las Salinas is a fervently chaotic ritual. Everyone eats and drinks, but most of all they make a lot of noise. They stoke the fires with screams as if they knew of no other way, tirelessly pounding drums. A group of us, sixteen or eighteen, got together to eat grilled chicken that Feli had brought from La Gamba Loca. We had more than enough beer. We also had corn on the cob that we roasted in the embers. When someone grabbed one of the smoking husks, they stood up and crossed the dark sand, now cooled by the night, and went down to the water. They threw the corn into the sea and, taking their time, they let the water swirl around their ankles waiting for the tide to bring it back. They picked it up, shook off the water, and ate it. Delicious, with the perfect amount of salt. Back at the bonfire, we tried to agree on whether we should write wishes for three things we wanted and three things we didn't want for ourselves on two different pieces of paper. And if we threw one of the lists into the fire, what would we do with the one we didn't burn that night? Feli was glowing as he tried to negotiate a unanimous decision amid the din. I was a mess from the charcoal while he was impeccable in his Macael whites. In the end, of course, everyone did what they thought best. I wrote three wishes, two of them included you, and I put them in my pocket, intending to pull them out again on next year's solstice. Then I could burn them together with whatever else I didn't want in my life. I crumpled

21

up the other piece of paper and threw it hard into the flames. Feli's mother died on a night of San Juan. He mourns in white. Strictly. The liturgy ends with all the beach people in the water, swaying back and forth at their own rhythm. They enter the water running or walking. The children do forward flips splashing the older women. Everyone shouts to demonstrate to the world and to San Juan himself that this is a reverence, a show, a cult, a resolution, and a celebration. Some dive into the water and swim. Others, just ankle deep, splash water on the backs of their necks. But all, without exception, wait to be struck by three waves, then leave the water, slowly, walking backwards.

TEN
YOU WOULD HAVE FOLLOWED ME ANYWHERE

Once you sat on the washing machine. You had taken off your pants and looked like you were wearing a bikini, on a beach, seated, dipping your feet in the water from a rock. I sucked on them. I took your big toe in my mouth. I licked your soles and ran my tongue along the outside edge of your toes. I worked my way up your glistening shin. Rising from the water, I dried myself on your thighs like a pup, splashing you. I could see how the goosebumps rose on your skin in waves. Finally, I buried myself. I buried my face in your infinity, slipping your bikini to the side. You supported yourself with your hands, arcing backwards. You faced upwards, waiting for the sun to move across the kitchen ceiling, above the washing machine. You didn't sound like someone sunbathing. I slowly untied the string of your swimsuit and quickly entered you. I savored your entire life, and those short, tight gasps. I raised your legs slightly with my shoulders. You followed me. You would have followed me anywhere. I rested my cheek against your inextinguishable heat and nibbled your thigh. The muscles all through your body contracted deliciously. I returned. One always returns. I opened my mouth and offered you my tongue. You tensed up, again and again. Then the taste of metal returned. It was there somewhere. I remembered that taste in your mouth and the symptoms coursed through me. It was in no specific place on my tongue. I tasted it a little here, a little there. Abruptly, I straightened up, and as quickly as I could, resumed my interrogation of your tongue. I discovered nothing. I fell once again to my knees and searched. I found something. I grasped your legs and pulled them towards me. You balanced your body on the corner edge of the washer, perched on your butt. You gripped the edge of the washer like a raptor. You were still staring into the sun, with your eyes closed, lips dry, mouth open, stifling your voice. I didn't stop until you dissolved into me.

ELEVEN
DECISIONS, DECISIONS

"So, which board do you think would be good for me?"

"Wet are you?"

"Regular." This means that I stand with my left foot forward, toward the nose.

"No, no, I mean your sign." Sometimes I didn't understand Eric, but not because of his accent.

"Huh?"

"Oh, sheet, Leo, Pisces…" Eric was easily irritated when not in the water.

"Oh, no idea."

"Where do you sairf?"

"Wherever they let me." Anywhere and everywhere you can go and see waves. Traveling with a board rather than a pretext is the best way I know.

"Oo-la-la!, mon ami."

When he asked me what I liked to do in the water the conversation took off. For Eric, this wasn't just a way of life, it's that outside of this there isn't anything else. We spoke about maneuvers, tricks, styles. Some guys showed up who wanted to nose about Eric's workshop and I used the opportunity to go and get two *leche y leche* coffees.

"What kind of music do you like?"

"What?"

"You like music, non? Tell me what you like, what do you leessen to on zee radio?"

I started naming a list, which he cut short. Immediately he asked me what I thought came after death, if I would be satisfied if I died today, if I thought that one day they would develop a system for taking the dance out of us. If I was right or left handed, if I considered myself more of a happy penguin with his own kind, or, on the contrary, a solitary eagle circling the sky, stalking its prey.

"*Bien*, after all zat and having seen you sairf, you have several opshunz." Eric put his glasses back on the tip of his nose, crinkling it up.

"Although I recommend zis one for you," he grabbed the board the way a father accompanies his daughter to the altar. Eric had just finished a six'three, recently glazed and cured, all set to go. He stared at me through his bifocals, opening his heart. He seemed to regret what he'd just said. In spite of everything, he took a deep breath, he set what we already knew was going to be *my* board delicately on the floor, and looked for a cigarette in his shirt pocket, which was smeared with resin.

We stared at each other, pretending not to, but still staring. She lay on her side in all her roundness and fragility, and we dissolved into one another. Her double concave mischievously offering herself, her dimensions, her lines, suggesting everything without saying a word, her sharp edges, the rise of her ass.

Fourteen
Bottled Up

"Señora, we're about to take off, you'll have to turn that off immediately," Stevenson's hands were sweating.

"But I can't," her English was pinched and hard at the edges. Her eyes, blue and cold. She handed it to him to see if he could. It took him a moment to recognize the device. It wasn't the latest cellphone, or a mini console, or a tablet. It was a tamagotchi. It had been a while since he'd seen one of those puppies, and never on a flight.

"Do you know how to turn it off?"

"Nope," he turned it over, expecting to find a switch. As he examined the yellow pup, the woman grabbed another tamagotchi from her youngest daughter. The two girls looked up, their eyes glazed. There were probably three or four minutes left before takeoff. He absorbed the sweat with a napkin, drops had sprung up with reminders of the previous night. He went back and joined the rest of the crew.

"They have two tamagotchis."

"No shit!"

"Two what?"

"Two tamagotchis. It's like an electronic egg. You have to take care of it to keep it alive."

"She says you can't turn them off."

"I think they die if you don't feed them." Stevenson walked back to his passengers, flipping the hair back from his forehead with a practiced snap that sprang from his neck.

"Excuse me, Madame, we're about to take off. All electronic devices must be turned off, so we have to dispose of them."

"Oh, my god!"

The mother anticipated the consequences of his words, the girls shifted their wide open gazes from their tamagotchis to

26

the flight attendants, without quite understanding, but sensing looming tragedy. They seemed resigned to their execution. They studied them carefully, but there was no way to turn them off. The airbus engines revved, and they returned the electronic eggs to their owners, because in the course of their training they had been instructed on how to discern urgency from emergency. They held their posts until after take-off. Then Stevenson approached the passengers again. They wouldn't meet his gaze, whereas he found it impossible not to glance at the mother's cleavage, covered with freckles. He brought them three bottles of mineral water with plastic glasses and ice. All on a tray decorated with napkins emblazoned with the Company logo. It was out of inertia that he was trying to be nice. He smiled at them, saying, "What luck," trying to win them over, without much success, grinning through his teeth. "This trip the electronic devices are pardoned."

But the mother was quite overcome by anxiety and distress. One of the little girls was crying, the other stared at her family, coddling the little yellow pup in her delicate hands. Stevenson explained to them again that any device could interfere with the plane's navigation system. This was also something they were taught in their training, though no one really believed it. He explained to them that they were used to carrying that kind of cybernetic passenger, that they weren't considered in any of the manuals, and that perhaps it would be better not to feed them during the week of vacation they were just beginning, perhaps they shouldn't care for them at all. He wondered aloud whether they had a resurrection function, whether they were only granted one life. Stevenson could be very funny. Although he was a native speaker with impeccable English, it wasn't very orthodox and was probably incomprehensible to a Scandinavian housewife. Now the mother, after taking a long drink of water, with teary eyes the size of Easter eggs, tried clumsily to protect her children by covering their ears.

"So, you want me to kill them now?"

FIFTEEN
WE LOOKED AT EACH OTHER

We stared at each other. Pretending not to, but still staring. Surrounded by people, almost all of them naked, it didn't matter to us, because we were staring at each other. You and I were also naked. At El Charquito, the whole world was naked, some lying in the sun, others swimming. You and I, getting hot, staring at each other, pretending not to.

Without clothing you were a sculpture. I supposed that dressed you'd look even better. You moved with cautious elegance, you seemed to be all alone in the world. Alone and nude with your long legs, exposed hips, highlighted bikini lines. You were reading or, at least, you held a book in your hands and when I looked at you I could sense your absolute calm. You stood up and walked towards the shore of El Charquito, extending your funambulist arms to keep your balance as you stepped over the rocks on your way down to the sea. You looked towards the horizon, thinking. Everyone, men and women, watched you go down to the water along the volcano cable. The women envied you, the men desired you, and I watched. I stood up and I too walked towards the shore to be near you, convincing myself I was just making up with the sea, which was as flat as a soup dish. I stood at the edge, perhaps to confront the sea, face to face, and reproach her for not delivering a single one of the promised waves. To reproach her for the gouges in my board thanks to the rocks a few days back, to make a request, to speak to her, but most of all to see you up close.

Now, just two meters apart, we looked at each other, and no matter how hard I tried, I couldn't tear my eyes away from yours which, by comparison, made the turquoise clarity of El Charquito seem gloomy. We smiled at each other, unable to avoid it. I sat on a rock, with one leg in the water, bending the other so

I could kneel on one leg, feeling for something on the bottom, some algae, or something so I could stop looking at you. My nudity seemed to expand thanks to my cavernous flesh.

"How did you do that?" Your voice was palm oil.

"Eh?" Now I dove into the water, to distract your gaze from unwelcome changes in my physique, and in so doing splashed you a little. In vain, you tried to protect yourself with your hands and then assumed a pose like Marilyn over the subway grate, but without the white dress.

"I'm sorry."

"No problem, I was going to swim too. What did you do to your foot?"

My toe had a scab from a previous injury which, having soaked it over and over in sea water and applied and removed numerous band-aids, now had the appearance of an emergency.

"Oh, this? I fell." As you bent down and felt the water with your hand, I glanced at your body, head to toe. I was at the base of a statue. Your legs were the eternal antechamber to Brazilian infinity, your navel a mandatory stop before arriving at your breast, rising to greet the sun.

"On a motorcycle?"

"No. Surfing."

You made a disappointed sound, kind of smacking your lips.

"Oh, okay, you're a slider."

"Well, more or less." (That word is horrible, but yes.) "I'm one of those who, if he can, goes to the beach with his toy under his arm."

"Surfers are cool," you said, listlessly. It took me two weeks to convince you I wasn't longing to die my hair blond, that what I had was an affliction and that if treated properly, three or four surfs per week, I was able to lead a practically normal life. Surfing seems to me to be more of an intoxicant than a sport, a statement or a lifestyle. A drug without tolerance, which always manifests with plenitude, always like the first time. It never saturates, is never excessive, and it's hangover only causes regret, if only a little, in making you go just that much farther, always a little more.

"Well, the thing is, I have an affliction that requires that I swim whenever the sea moves."

"Have you seen a doctor?"

When it started to get dark we dressed and you touched my wound. I asked you endless questions, seeking an answer, any answer. You drank one martini after another to polish the glow in your eyes. They distilled the rainbow, captured the essence of all the colors combined, a bottomless pit, a lush marsh, an empty bottle of wine.

Sixteen
The Stillness of Junk

I ran into Eric on the boardwalk that goes down to the beach. It's a strategic lookout point. Studying the bay from there, you can evaluate the current, the cadence of the waves, their volume and the number of surfers in the water. If there are few, if there are many, if they are the sons of this rootedness to a land filled with the shit of dogs and cigarette butts. Many don't even get out of their cars. They park at the overview and evaluate the sea through tinted windshields, with the motor running, drowned out by a monochord baseline saturated with low notes. There are those who make their decision with binoculars in hand, those who don't even need to get that close to decide, and those who once they've put their board under their arm turn their head this way and that, catching a glimpse of a slanted sunset or orange clouds, and they go back home. I'm going down because, even though you can see a current, it doesn't look strong and I have to try out my new board. Eric is smoking with the air of a condemned man. He shakes my hand and lights me a cigarette, bristling with white shavings from polishing fiber. He was so sardonic that when a group of tourists—from the Pyrenees, like me—passed by, he glanced at me with a crooked smile, and said to them very quickly, to hide his accent, "Can you dance zee duck?" After furrowing their brows, trying to make sense of the question, the three of them said, in unison, "Quoi?" He looked at me again, now impassive, and then answered them in sophisticated French. Eric sees things very clearly. At his age he says he prefers quality over quantity. He basically opts to be non-categorical, but when he sees me carrying the new board and an obvious silly grin, he lights up.

"I'm trying it out today!"

"I'll come with you."

Before beginning the descent along the dirt and stone path, littered with trash, odd sandals and abandoned underwear, he points out to me, stressing his words on the final syllable, that at the bottom, along with the rocks at The Sewer, there is an immense and new rock, shiny and black.

"'ave you seen it?"

"No, I haven't had a good look at it, Eric, but now that I see it, that's the smashed up wreck of a car."

It had run off the highway in the direction of the beach, no other possibility. It fell forty meters. Saturday nights…, (insert here the name of some well-known place, for example, The Sewer…), people take drugs, and the curves of this serpentine highway along the coast become a play-station screen. According to reports, at daybreak on Sunday, the car was there. There were four people and the coroner took all four of them. The car went out of control and the brakes froze up, catapulting the car up and over the guardrail of fifty centimeters, which remained intact, and through a hole in the crash barrier, then, a drop of forty meters to the beach.

As you wait in the water, it is astonishing to look towards the car. You're overcome by a morbid attraction, your mouth dropped open. The stillness of junk embedded in the sand only recalls the virulence of the entire process that led to its being there. It was black with tinted windows, now the wreck is a gem without sparkle embedded in a quarry. It will be there until the end of winter.

SEVENTEEN
CROOKNOSE

It wasn't the words that came from his mouth, which were cleverly muffled by distance and the splash of his strokes and, so, were indecipherable when they reached me. Nor was it his well-studied image of an extra in an American TV series, the bad-guy-bank-robber type, or imposing airport security guard, depending on the channel. An accident, probably a confrontation with a wild school of monk sharks in Maui, or very simply a hard punch by some nervous guy, had reshaped his facial rictus, transforming him into a kind of rabid mental case for the rest of his days, and that ultimately has an impact. It was, more than anything, the bitter odor of bile rotting in his entrails like eggs rotting in the sun. For that reason, I turned and looked at him with commiseration and repugnance, in asymmetric proportions.

It started to become evident that the idiot with the big mouth was addressing me. He had just crossed into my personal space and, what's worse, he was sputtering in my direction, apparently upset, as he unleashed his poetry. I was just getting into the water but had yet to get completely wet. I hadn't even had time to offend him yet.

"You fucking barbarian, you *godo*! Get the hell out of here, you son of a whore. I'm sick of all of you!" His sneer was so wide, his rippling gums exposed.

"What are you saying?" My accent must have driven him crazy and earned me top spot in his catalog of hate.

"I shit on your whore of a mother. Where are you from, huh? Tell me, where are you from?"

"What do you care?" (Where I'm from we crucify people like you in our living rooms. We smack your faces with open hands. Shit like you doesn't end up in the sea, it's converted into fertilizer. For us, traveling is a commodity and borders are for ridiculous redneck jokes like you.) I tried to be polite since the whole thing must have been some kind of mistake. In any case, the guy looked familiar but I didn't know from where.

"What do I care? You don't know who I am, do you? You got into a scrap with me the other day at the airport, or don't you remember? You don't know who you're talking to, you foreign shit. Get out of here, I don't want to see you anymore, this is my spot, my beach, my wave, my people, my ocean, my island, and we don't want any stinking foreigners here. Don't make me have to tell you again."

The waves were passing over the swimmers and their boards, all aware of the scene but responding with different attitudes. Astonishment and discomfort were apparent in the majority of the faces, but three of them were watching with malicious smiles, poised to become part of the scene at any moment, whenever the rabid one gave the signal. "Before we weren't in a disco but here and now you're in the wrong place!"

"Then I guess we have a little problem, *compadre.*"

"No, it's you who's got a big problem, gringo. And don't even talk to me, you folks don't even have a right to talk, go back to your own piece-of-shit country." The shouting brought out the veins in his eyeballs, as my eager fist flexed beneath the water, and I mapped out different possible scenarios as I sought the quickest route between my knuckles and his second-hand nose. For a moment, I imagined the fight in the water and the beating I'd get from Crooknose's three friends, scandal in the bay, lumps of clotted blood in the sand; a have-you-seen poster with my picture on it, pinned to a wall for years, next to other ones saying Locals Only at the entrance to the beach. The tip of his board touched my leg and, after taking a deep breath, glancing at the highest peak on The Island, which happens to be covered with snow today, for which reason it exuberantly reflects the blues of the sky, I set myself in position. I stopped him with the same hand I hoped to use to shatter his face, his intentions and his monotonous discourse.

"You can say all that without touching me, right champ?"

To hesitate is not the way of the locals, but this guy wasn't exactly an aborigine. Blond, Aryan aspect, a Teuton grandson of some ambulance driver for the Third Reich in the Great War II who, after the surrender, fled all the way to this place. Nor did he spend his whole life sleeping in the sand at The Sewer, nor was he even sure of what he was doing right now. Perhaps he spoke too much or too loudly. In any case, he looked for answers from his three hefty and bleached-blond buddies, pumped with steroids at their trusted gymnasium, backing him up with arms crossed over their boards at a minimum distance. While Crooknose lashed out at me I watched their eyes as they shrugged their shoulders, looking down at the water, trying to spot some bream or rock fish with an answer in its mouth. Their stupidity tinted the sea a pale pink, and caused a few heartbeats to race. I ground my teeth out of anger but stayed in the water, more nihilist than stoical.

"I'm not going to tell you again, you stinking *godo*, get out of the water." Those were his last words up close to me before the circumstances changed and his congestion and a stream of tears caused him to sputter. I wasn't going to leave so long as I didn't want to. I shouted, "Bacaguaré!" which is a word in Guanche, a language he doesn't know, meaning, "I want to die," and was used as a battle cry. I glared back at the fragile stares of the Cretin Xtreme Team. He insisted, at a distance of a few strokes away from me, that he had warned me of the consequences. Slowly he drew further away, muttering and escorted by his friends who paddled energetically and now began to threaten me from a distance. I heard him telling them about the scene at the airport and they shook their heads, looking at me condemningly, and he pointed his finger as if to say, " hold-me-back-or-I'll-kill-him." I stayed in the water for a couple more hours and, as for Crooknose, I turned him into a pillar of salt so he wouldn't bother me anymore but, to tell you the truth, the swim just wasn't the same.

He'd get out, sooner or later.

EIGHTEEN
DUKE PAHOA KAHINO MOKOE
HULIKOHOLA KAHANA MOKU

Duke Pahoa Kahino Mokoe Hulikohola Kahana Moku was sucking his finger, trying to stem the bleeding. As soon as he set foot in Sidney, with a small suitcase of wrinkled leather, and his hands in his pockets, just a few weeks earlier, he found a good tree to his liking and asked for an axe. He chopped it down, peeled off the bark, and from an elongated section of the trunk he shaped it until he gave it the form he wanted for an enormous board. Four and a half meters long, fifty-two kilos. With the work done, a horrendous pain went straight through to his heart, from his heart finger. He didn't need fins, they hadn't been invented yet. Nor had the leash for connecting the board to the body of the rider so as not to lose it in case of a fall. That's how they made boards in Olo, Hawaii, and he was far from home. He was quite a traveler, not bad for an islander. Now the bay at Sydney had filled with curious spectators who had learned of him over the years through the newspapers. Duke Pahoa Kahino Mokoe Hulikohola Kahana Moku had gained fame in the water of a pool and the name of Big Kahuna. He won several medals in different swimming events in consecutive Olympics. Stockholm 1912, 1920, and Paris 1924. During one of the finals his teammates had to wake him. He'd fallen asleep in the locker room, using a towel as a pillow. He went into the stadium, excused himself with upturned palms at the starting blocks, and proceeded to win the race. In another final, winning the silver medal, he was beaten by the most famous Tarzan in film history. After that, the world was submerged in the First World War, thus cancelling the next Olympics in which the Big Kahuna could have repeated his victories. Two days before Christmas '21, Duke Pahoa Kahino Mokoe Hulikohola Kahana Moku put on his blue and white striped swimsuit and went out on the waves towards that distant line above the sea that blurs with the horizon. The lifeguards at the beach gathered in a group to convince him that it was not the right time to go in the water. They'd spotted shark fins through their binoculars, which they carried with them to the tops of their tall chairs. He just smiled, his strong Hawaiian arms holding the part of the board that was not anchored in the sand. He gazed out along the horizon and didn't seem to hear them, until, after a minimal show of acknowledgment, nodding his head and arching an eyebrow, he expressed due respect for their information and then entered the water. Those present were consumed by an idiotic sense of panic. Gasps, eyes as wide as dinner plates, disproportionate exclamations, as that man, with the statuesque physique of a bronze general victoriously astride a horse, entered the water. Stretched out on the remains of the tree whose severed roots still tried to comprehend water and the substrata of the bay, began to paddle toward the ocean's breakers. For more than three hours Duke Pahoa Kahino Mokoe Hulikohola Kahana Moku flirted with the water. The newspapers published sepia-colored photos and dedicated an entire page to descriptions of this practically mythological man, despite the blue and white stripes of his enormous swimsuit. As he came out of the water, the lifeguards crowded around him, their first-aid kits open, prepared for anything, but Duke Pahoa Kahino Mokoe Hulikohola Kahana Moku was refreshed, content, and intact. They bombarded him with questions about the sharks to which he merely commented that he had seen many.

One of the lifeguards managed to ask him, "And didn't they bother you?"

"No," he answered. "But I didn't bother them either." The lifeguard, awed by the man's energy but seeing his mutilated finger, was certain that such a wound had to have been the work of one of the sharks. In the retelling of those events, the contribution of this detail helped forge the living legend of the man before their eyes. In this way, surfing was presented to the elegant and distant world, like the panic of certain dreams. Duke Pahoa Kahino Mokoe Hulikohola Kahana Moku gave to Australia and, by extension, to the entire world, another raison d'etre for the waves licking its coasts, and a reason to celebrate them, to enjoy and revere them. Duke Pahoa Kahino Mokoe Hulikohola Kahana Moku said that outside of the water he was nothing. His biographers describe him as a calm and quiet man on land, transparent and contained as the Pacific Ocean. A giant who walked the earth like a shadow. Regarding his death, the details remain unclear. Officially, only the passage of time could subdue his spirit. Nonetheless, several lines of investigation reveal that the family decided to keep his death quiet so that the persona would continue its domination of the person. There is evidence that at the age of seventy-eight he traveled as a passenger aboard the Queen Elizabeth VI, crossing the Atlantic. On a beautiful sunny day, with the rolling waves of the sea in the background singing softly into his ears, he went swimming in the small pool on the deck of the ocean liner. The ridiculousness of that scenario and the confirmation of his imminent decomposition led to his ultimate disappearance.

NINETEEN
WE ALWAYS GO BACK

I went back to the beach, we always go back. A jumble of treacherous waves stretched across the bay. The water was cold, a kind of warning, the sun was poking out from behind a couple of bloated clouds. I got into the water, I always go in, and when the storm started to take a don't-say-I-didn't-warn-you form, I caught some waves that will forever live on in some intangible place of memory. Naked, I walked around in the sand until my things had dried. I drew close to the car that lay dashed on the rocks. It was still in the same place, although losing its luster. The sand and salt slowly eating away at the metallic paint. People crawl around it taking pictures of the black tangled mess. An elegant way to portray the dead. Some take a souvenir with them, a piece of the dashboard, a rear-view mirror. The children climb all over it, barefoot, pretending to die on the highway, even pretending to be driven away in an ambulance. Two boys plant a couple of seats in a corner of the beach, torn from the rear of the car. They smoke, juggle, and lean their butts against the remains. Their legs are coated in gray sand. When the cliffs block the waning light behind them, they drag the seats to where the gently rising tide can't reach them.

TWENTY
GO DANCING?

You called, in a tizzy. You said you would come by my house right away. You asked my shoe size. I fantasized you were going to give me a pair of sweet yellow and green half-cabs. I figured you must have heard me talking about them at some time. You showed up with some dark, shiny shoes, with laces and leather soles. Even worse, they resembled my work shoes, though more pretentious and much less comfortable. You were wearing a tight skirt, really showing your curves, and open-toed high-heeled shoes. Your toenails matched the flowers on your T-shirt, which you had fastened in such a way as to cruelly expose your belly-button.

"We're going dancing."

"Where?" I blinked my eyes.

"Dancing, I need a partner." You smiled like a Chinese fortune cat. I remembered what Stevenson said, over and over, "Understand women? Oh, no, no, no, come on, you're mistaken. If you like a woman, stay with her as long as you can." From what I could tell, that was the most interesting thing his father had ever said.

"A partner? What kind of partner?"

"A dance partner. I signed up for tango classes and I want you to be my partner."

"But I've never danced tango in my friggin' life."

"Yea, but I've seen you dance the night away and, even though you're out of control, you're not half bad."

I gulped for air. This was going to be complicated. My idea of dancing has something more to do with drinking, wearing sunglasses, getting buzzed, a bunch of DJs, and a moderately high risk of having breakfast hundreds of kilometers from home. You were serious about dancing, for real, learning a technique, memorizing choreography, getting into a routine, spending time in a room with mirrors, surrounded by other couples, having an instructor dressed in sweats, wearing dance shoes.

You say *"Che, boludo!"* in your best Argentine Spanish as I rush around, grabbing the gel to slick my hair back. I slide across the freezing floor tiles, like a rattlesnake caressing the desert sand. Shhh, shhh, shhh. I guide you from one side of the dance floor to the other, I lean into your eyes just in time to watch as they lose their glimmer and the fluorescent lights in the room flicker, trying not to blackout. I support your back and watch your feet become entangled with mine, deceiving, disdaining, beckoning from one tile to another, from one measure to the next.

Now I'm feeling good and, what is worse, I feel like a good guy. Clean, clear, and powerful as melting water. You seem to have caught the fever. Hidden between your neck and your smile, you say nothing. You're magic, but you're not a trick or an illusion. You're invisible glitter, fleeting flavor, which is why your guardian angel exterminates.

You call me hurricane, you say my name is the name of a natural disaster, a cataclysm. I fill my chest with air and would love to lick your shoulders, blow on them, and level everything in my path.

You call me ballsy because I put on sunblock stolen from big box stores. I'll prove you right when I take you by the hand to rob the central bank. We'll dance in front of the frozen stares of our volunteer hostages. Then we'll brashly stroll out the front door with the booty in a bag. Whatever doesn't fit, we'll throw from the rooftop before making our getaway.

I feel good, and that's your fault.

Twenty-one
Chicho

The sea brought him everything with its convulsions. On the shore, he sorted through what had been churned up from its entrails. Those were the conditions. It had been a long time since Chicho possessed anything, or anyone, other than his nine-foot board of balsam wood, a record player and sometimes a few cold beers. When he named himself the new king and sole governor of his own life, at the age of thirty-some years, he had a vast reign, without belongings, and long hair that still hung below his shoulders, albeit laced with gray. In the aftermath of the storm of seventy-eight, his family was left with nothing more than an embankment where there had once been a house, now swept away. Built in a hurry, it crumbled in the mud. Just so they wouldn't immediately forget what they had once owned, the bank let them keep making payments for years. Long years. Chicho was small, which his father, sniggering and chugging beer, always joked had to do with the size of Chicho's nuts. Anyway, Chicho looked for a good location, with firm ground, beyond the mudslides. When he found the right place, he took his time, orienting it toward the sea, like an altar to an image. He chose Quemada Beach, or Quemada Beach chose him. It had witnessed his birth, had seen him tossed around by the waves, and spending hours brushing the sand from his balls, which was a lot of work. He had learned to swim there, and to catch his first squid. There, he had lost his fear of water, and of a few women. The beach had seen him almost drown a few times, but it had always saved him. That was long before they paved the road. And it was long before it occurred to anyone to set up a beach bar, which was only frequented by German retirees in socks and sandals, punctually every Monday, Tuesday and Friday, and scattered through the rest of the week, where they

43

would eat rock fish, usually brought by Chicho, freshly caught. Long before all this, he chose a sunny spot on a gentle slope and waited. Waited until the Atlantic brought him wood and ropes. Furniture yanked from the cabins of fishing boats, abandoned to some dark fate. Old clothes in cardboard boxes that floated into the bay. Then, when he tried to sell them by weight in some shop, after drying everything on the patio, he realized that what he thought were old rags had now come back into fashion. Bundles of merchandise in poor shape to unload, without pain or glory, on the healthy black market. Plastic bags, hardly used life-preservers and some gifts that were difficult to accept from the ocean, such as a stuffed moose head, which he used for a while as a coat rack and then gave away as soon as he could, mortified that anyone would actually want such a thing. It didn't take him long to build a hut, which is the main room of his house to this day. Besides adding on with irregular wood walls and gypsum roofs, he put in a gas camp stove and a cot. Everyone who who's been there knows him and everyone who lives in the area knows that he forms part of the ecosystem. Chicho offers to the world his gaunt face—the lookout atop the mainmast—his cutting sniper's comments—perched in a tower close to a park on a Sunday morning, and a collection of stories the ocean has left scattered across the sand, mixed in with the trash. In exchange, he asks for nothing. He takes it. This authorizes Chicho to always be on the verge of pouncing on something. Small and sinewy like Iggy Pop, not so striking, but all rats flee, even from house cats. The walls of his house are covered from floor to ceiling with three thousand stickers. Eric, when he came back to The Island, spent a month there, listening to Chicho, bringing him beer, doing the shopping, dipping prickly pears in *gofio* as the tide went out, and losing himself in the bay whenever he could. Eric was from one of those villages that don't show up on any Atlas, which is why he had a French passport, an accent, and an island child. After five years on The Island, he decided to go back to France with his son. Nostalgia for the land; at least, that's what he thought. He made good boards and the gig worked out, but eventually he came to realize that The Island beckoned him in his dreams. Taking his son by the hand and a board under his arm, he returned, appealing to Chicho for asylum. That's when he counted the stickers. Three thousand thirteen stickers covering the plywood room partitions. Three thousand thirteen swatches of color, the first of which had been stuck to the wall close to the floor, in a corner behind a mattress recently dried under the setting sun. After that it only took four years to cover the rest of the walls, a ton of friends, tourists, companions and acquaintances. The word got around that if you brought Chicho something to drink and some stickers, the door to his hut would always be open. On his walls coexist advertisements for skateboards, supermarkets, surf boards, bands, World Cup logos, Use Caution warnings, grapefruits, bars and any piece of paper or plastic designed to adhere. Underlying the odors of the house, butts in the ashtray, banana peels in the garbage, neoprene, scented wax, dirty laundry and dishes, there is an overpowering aroma of vinyl.

TWENTY-TWO
FORESIGHT

Stevenson's father is, of course, a British subject. He has flocks
of swallow tattoos from his forearms to the backs of his hands,
and he visits Stevenson every winter. He manages to make Stevenson's life impossible, justified by their familial bonds, and
he signs up for all the excursions offered to foreign retirees.
Stevenson lives on The Island, although he was born on the
mainland. He got married in Epicentro and now his ex-wife is
trying to sell a house on the outskirts of the city. He likes the
beach, he wouldn't know how to live without it anymore, although he scarcely knows how to swim. He dreams of getting
up the courage to learn how to scuba dive. At the moment he's
fishing with a rod from the shore and he wonders if he isn't too
old for just about everything. The episode of the tamagotchis,
that all happened to Stevenson. He's a flight attendant. So am
I—since a few months ago—so I have to put on my work shoes,
smile for sixteen straight hours and wear perfume. Stevenson
says that this wave business is not for epicureans because it begins in the exact same place where you leave your car. Without
a car, it's difficult to find waves, so the freedom that's associated
with surfing is restricted by the need for a vehicle that, at the
very least, has lots of space and, sometimes, all its documents
in order. It's possible to spend an entire morning looking for a
small beach where the waves wash in at uneven intervals. To
get there, you really have to pay close attention to the end of
the newscasts. You have to study the local reports. So, ignore
the gunshots, mortar rounds and desperate, fly-ridden children.
Rush past politicians who look like film artists, film artists who
aspire to play gunslingers and then, there at the end, comes the
weather report. To try to grant credibility to this guy, who looks
so nice with his colorful tie and, between jokes, points out an

anticyclone in Finisterre and describes the ice storms in the highlands, while I'm here wondering why he doesn't just use a cardboard map like everybody else, instead of some complex system of projections on a white backdrop. Then, when he signs off, lifting his designer glasses and waving them in one hand, he looks more like a clown than a scientist and you wonder if this guy has ever seen a heliograph or a hygrometer in his entire life, or if he thinks a Stevenson's screen is a flight steward's new flat-screen TV. Sun or clouds, south or east wind, swell or tsunami. Then, in privacy, I imagine I'm some kind of wind guru, and I scan the internet and consult a tide table. After all this, I'm still only able to make some feeble prediction, which the sea, the wind, and the land—the true living forces—will undermine because I will have overlooked something. Now I've succeeded in bringing my van to a frothing-at-the-mouth coastline. I'm a little closer to becoming a prophet. Later I'll become an amphibian enveloped in lycra and neoprene. A cold-blooded and clumsy amphibian who would do anything for a complete set of gills and who walks on tiptoes when barefoot because of the prickly pebbles beneath the soles of my feet. Going barefoot from my car is the best thing to do, with nothing else in hand than my gear and my keys. Sometimes you see adult crybabies going from one end of the beach to the other, hair wet and their hands in the air, looking for their knapsacks, their glasses, their bags and keys. You should only carry your essentials when you go to the beach if you plan to go into the water. And then there's the key to the van. It's important to know where you left it, because you have to discreetly leave everything else in your vehicle, which is what the big crybaby lost. I sometimes hang it from my neck with a string while swimming, like the key to a chastity belt. Sometimes I look for a rock that is easy enough to relocate, far enough from the beach, which the tide won't steal forever, and I put my trust in fate. Sometimes, from the water, while everyone's talking about some great maneuver, or the Maldive

Islands, and they're all salivating on each other's shoulders, you can see smart-ass kids in baseball caps, with just shaved, dragon-tattooed legs, anxiously turning over rocks. And then more rocks. Then, with the sought-after prize in hand they run and try their luck in the locks of the cars parked along the sidewalk bordering the beach. First one, then another, then another.

Twenty-three
Pancho

It was a show of linguistic invention that led the reporter to call him a big fish with no financial worries. Some readers laughed at the idea. Nineteen thousand hits on google under his name, forty kilos, and more or less the same number of years, more than the most famous grouper in Mar de La Calma. That's why he's a bit of a show-off, a tad exhibitionist, and quite spoiled. Pancho lets himself be photographed in return for food, he almost always lets people touch him, although he's never let himself be trapped by furtive submarines. He's been speared several times and he's been seen with hooks in his mouth, but this has never been enough to haul him from the water. He's a salty-dog measuring more than a meter and a half in length. Since we insist on dressing our mascots in overcoats, whenever we can, the local photographers and scuba divers tried to find him a girlfriend. Natalia, a precious female with voluptuous glistening scales. A spear gun nailed Natalia one day in a clear sea. There was great mourning and clothing was shredded as cries filled the sky. Pancho kept a straight grouper face in spite of it all. Out of respect, the hotel keepers on the coast decided not to serve grouper to the patrons. Instead, they prepared a great celebration, since they were sure Pancho would reach a half century in age. When that happens, there are those who would like to celebrate with great revelry, while others plan an assassination, followed by taxidermy, and they'd like to hold the honors in the Commodore's Hall at the sunniest hotel on the coast.

Twenty-four
Bring Me the Sea

"I've never seen the sea." Aurora had been coming to the lottery kiosk every Thursday for almost a year and a half.

"Oh, no?"

"No. In fact I've only been to Villaverde, which is where I was born. Here, and the courthouse in Plaza de Castilla.

"Come on."

She smelled vaguely of toxins, sour perspiration, like a lot of the people who went there for methadone. She stopped by the kiosk every week hoping the blind man might bring her luck. Many came to the blind man for the same reason. Women returning from the market, the unemployed, former patients with discharge papers in hand, grief-stricken family members, and occasionally the workers on the methadone-bus would take half an hour off, more or less punctually at noon, and then they'd continue along their routes. The blind man had a good kiosk, very well located, next to the provincial hospital. Aurora cast a big shadow, she was a bit overweight. A good sign according to the therapists. It showed she wasn't shooting up and she was putting on weight again. Aurora also smelled of No More Tears, a fragrance she shared with her four-year-old son. She was coquettish, but not quite cut out to be. She told the blind man how she'd spent her life going from town to crack house, sleeping in burned out cars, and pushing drugs. Anything for some flake. Now she was making a huge effort and she had talent, a talent that had been hibernating for long years. Every week she smelled a little better. And she had switched from the muffled sound of running shoes to the tap-tap of low heels, comfortable and elegant, with her own style, which is how she announced her approach every Thursday a little before noon. A confidant, deliberate stride, and awkward at the same time, quick, with a slight drag. She limped a little on her right leg. The first time, she approached the kiosk very nervously. Later, Mario, the blind man, learned that she had just entered the program and that she was very serious about never shooting up again, mainly for her son's sake. She couldn't stand still and her sentences jumbled together, which is why he thought she'd come to rob him. He'd been robbed several times and, to discourage more robberies, and without theatricality, Mario applied whatever guile he had at his disposal. He spoke to her in the gruffest voice he could muster and he took off his sunglasses. He directed his gray eyes at Aurora, eyes that had been destroyed years ago, so that she could sense his amorphous, pale wounds. With his hands on the counter, his body leaning forward, the way some insects will do to frighten off their predators, he smiled with the cynical calm he had learned over time to form with his mouth. He was aware that Aurora was sweating profusely. She was unable to explain with any clarity the reason for her visit and left quickly when she heard the anxious squeal of her bus's brakes. That day it was running late. Fifteen minutes later, she came back. It had been a hot spring. They had been cutting the lawn near the entrance of the hospital garden. Aurora always carried a yellow plastic bag, rustling in her hand, from the supermarket on the corner where she and everyone else bought half-liter cans of beer. The empty cans then clattered as they were tossed onto the sidewalk. When she rested the bag on the counter, he heard plastic vials clattering against each other. Later, the blind man learned from Aurora that they contained her daily medications for the week. The bus drivers say only the ones who take vials home with them can be trusted. They are pretty much the only ones who aren't shooting up, don't stab each other for their pills, or sell Xanax to the addicts while waiting for the meth-bus. She asked for a ticket with a three on it, she didn't care about the order of the numbers. The blind man gave her 14853, which he knew was hanging on the strip between his left shoulder and the kiosk door. He gave it to

51

her without looking at it since, for Mario, it would either be a perfunctory or completely futile thing to do.

"How...?"

She remained as still as a wall, so the blind man charged her a couple of bills, topping off the trick with great effect: "It has a three, right?"

Aurora paid him, uttered wow, and since then she returned every Thursday to buy a ticket and chat.

"Well, I've also been in Yeserías penitentiary, in two different blocks, but that's like being nowhere at all."

Mario turned his head up to the sky. "In fact, I have seen the sea, but I don't remember it. That was a long time ago. I was a child. I don't remember it, or much of anything else from when I could see and my eyes were anything but decorations. What I do remember is the heat of those days on Canela Beach and how cold the water was. The crust of salt hardening on my skin until I washed it away with freshwater. The noise, the wonderful noise of the waves, constant, almost imperceptible during the day, but always there, accompanying my naps. I remember the orange color of my pail, brilliant, like your methadone. We would make sandcastles for hours only to stomp on them in an instant. The fragrance of seaweed tossed up by the sea, drying on the sand. The sand would get on us without our noticing and then it would be everywhere. You could find it in the car, running your hand over the seat, months after we'd returned from vacation. I also remember how delicious the cold potato tortilla was, my body still wet and my head snug inside a cap."

Aurora would have started to cry, had she been alone. The blind man had no tolerance for sympathy. Instead, she grimaced in a way that Mario could sense the darkness in her mouth, absent of teeth, having put so much shit in it. A mouth that had once been pretty. She told him she wanted to take her son, Adrián, to see the sea that summer, that she couldn't decide between the Mediterranean and the Atlantic. Mario remained

52

quiet, he felt incapable of explaining to someone the difference between an ocean and a sea. Aurora's voice had grown thin until whistling like a silent thread as she spoke of Adrián, their future, their beach, their beers with the sea up to their ankles.

"If I go, I'll bring you a little bit of the sea in a lunch box, I promise."

"Just promise me that you'll go, and when you're there, buy me a postcard, the ugliest one you can find. Instead of writing me anything, which someone would just have to read to me, the day you plan to return, put it in the water, roll it around in the sand, and let it absorb the beach. Bring it to me and I'll hang it up here in the kiosk."

Twenty-five
What Are You Waiting For?

I didn't have to push the button. It was enough to place my finger on the buzzer for the door to creak open. Suddenly you swung the door open, with a shawl draped over your shoulders. The room was lit with the flicker of hundreds of small candles. The light from behind you revealed that you weren't wearing anything underneath. You grabbed me by the T-shirt, dragged me inside, closed the door with your heel and I was lost.

You got me to come over by calling me on the phone, just when I was seriously trying to forget you. We had already gotten together too many times. I knew your house, I knew your circumstances, and from the first time I saw you, I had seen your body naked. But I still didn't know the taste of anvil in your mouth. I ran the risk of becoming your friend—I already had friends, men and women, some of whom made room for me in their beds—and I didn't want to get involved in asking you out for a drink. The idea of forgetting you seemed to make the most sense. Knowing that you were lovely and different, I could have focused on finding someone pretty and common, and longed for you when I couldn't sleep.

The afternoon before that night, on the beach, I made a show of the most despicable, perfect gentleman's manners. I watched the guys surfing right barrels, I swallowed saliva and beer in equal parts, and I used my skills of self-control not to leave you there with your friends, talking about other friends I didn't know, reminiscing over high school memories. I would have liked to get up and run to the van, grab my board, turn around and scamper past all of you, sending sand in all directions, heading for the shoreline, to smile once and just say goodbye, Indonesian-style. After a couple of fortuitous brushes of our hands and another session of unnecessary sincerity, I left you in your home. After slamming the car door and smiling at you, I said to myself, in a ventriloquist's voice, "Forget about her." I liked being with you too much, but the lovely fragrance that rose from your delicate skin was not meant to be tracked like a bloodhound, nor acknowledged with a raised glass, held between two fingers, by a sommelier. I wanted to snort it like a rock star on a big tour. But then, that same night, you called me again, shrill and irritated.

"Why didn't you kiss me when you left my house? What are you waiting for? How long will it take you to get here?"

Stevenson's father entered my head without knocking. "Oh, no, no, come on, don't try to understand them." It took me a little less than a rescue helicopter would have taken to cover the distance.

Twenty-six
Pro

Once again, chasing a set, which, in Cenitz, means just hanging out. Fun, but lazy. People who have never been anywhere else say that the problem is the breakwater. Before, an immense wave would swallow the entire beach. Where now there are small motorboats for Sunday floaters, fuel-oil lovers, and an occasional sailboat, the waves were once bucking broncos that couldn't be tamed. The sea bed is of pointed rocks, rabid: volcanic. A sharp sea bed, all along the calm beach. The slope is vicious and, if you wait patiently, you'll see at least one surfer come out with a broken board, eyes full of salt water, shimmering even more brightly than the surface of the sea. Cenitz has a seafront promenade where people often stop to watch the surfers, the maneuvers, the rolls, and what can actually be done with one of those boards they have stashed in their attics, which they so often see in the hands of champions and under the arms of good-looking hunks in advertisements. When Eric arrived, it was already late. The sun was about to disappear and he was met by a herd of tourists pestering the waves with their voices and flashing digital cameras. Click click zoom click zoom click click. If there were photographers, there were presumably pro(fessional)s and he was not pleased because when there are supposed pros, there are few pro(babilitie)s that it's worth the trouble to venture out. It's tenser out there than in a long-distance pissing contest and you end up having to settle for leftovers. They always come hungry, with their mouths open, and no one can stand them. Eric took his time getting his stuff ready. He was already considering it a wasted afternoon. The best thing to do was to just accept and enjoy the loss of time, money, and productivity of being. The sun was a distant but insistent threat of fire. Curvilinear women strolled by, abundant with motion and scanty of clothing, so he decided to wander off and get an orange and banana juice and returned prepared for the worst. The audience, as expected, was boisterous and vulgar, and all around them a cloud had formed composed of rising fumes of every possible variant on sunblock for sensible skin. Through his sunglasses Eric watched the Big Kahuna, the king of the peak for the moment. He was well-positioned and, although the wave wasn't much to get excited about, it kicked off a set that promised to be magnanimous, slowly opening in both directions. Big Kahuna lost the wave and the crown because he doubtfully paddled and it indifferently offered itself up in all its sensuality and serenity as if to a lover it knew too well, flirtatiously sending froth up to kiss the beach. Behind it came another with similar intentions. Five contenders slapped at the water instead of paddling. Their faces were constipated with fear, or, perhaps, a kind of respect. One of them lost it, while three of them, in a sophisticated show of asynchronicity, attempted to pop up. No turns, no daring, no style. Eric didn't understand. The audience was still there with fingers on the triggers of their cameras and holding their breath, hoping to release it in a collective howl. The response from the sea came from a few strokes beyond: a pod of dolphins was gleefully leaping in the big wave, now in its trough, the same defiant wave that not one surfer had managed to grab that afternoon. Six or seven glistening figures dove through the water, carving the wildest curves of the session, and then, yes, the congregation of tourists and gawkers unleashed their wave of oohs and ahhs, clicks, zooms, and wows. Eric glanced at the onlookers, the pros and cons, and was surprised to find himself contemplating the dolphins. Since he didn't want to seem wimpy, he put on his lycra and entered the water, feigning to have a go at the waves, actually just enjoying the view, astraddle his six'two, as the dolphins dove through one set after another.

We keep waiting. Sometimes for fifteen minutes between sets. We wait for however long is necessary. Which is why Cenitz is a social place. Even here, fifteen minutes without talking, surrounded by people bobbing in the sea, is a difficult test. Normally, questions abound about the waves on the sea the day before, the waves at high tide, what size board you're using. We were all enjoying Eric's story about the dolphins when someone said, shit, look at that. All our eyes followed the direction of his finger, pointing toward the horizon. Our laughter dropped into the water like fishing weights. A raft filled with standing and passive passengers floated by, towed by a Coast Guard tugboat. Perhaps they were watching us. They were being taken from one port to another. They had reached our coast a couple of days before and now they were being taken back in their own floating coffin, to save money, and most importantly to avoid leaving a bad taste with the inhabitants of the first world, for those of us there, but we didn't have to put up with that scene that was so familiar and certain to be on the television newscast at night. The tugboat moved slowly, mocking the raft, which was a kamikaze of naval engineering, and now, also, the executioner's wagon *en route* to the square. The guys began to run through their repertoire of shipwreck jokes with generic punchlines, shielded by our shared well-being. They laughed with the disgusting delight of certainty that nothing like this could ever happen to us. I commented that thinking with the ass can only produce shit, that nothing prevented their mortgages from deciding to bite the hands that jacked them off. I got out of the water, riding a benign wave that gently accompanied me to the shore. It was a delicious afternoon with a shy breeze blowing to perfection. I left a trail of sulfurous smoke in the sand. I dried off with the old coca-cola towel I only use on the beach. I took off my cheap watch—waterproof, shockproof, with alarm and calendar. From the shore I threw rocks at Eric and the others, who were still laughing. If the rocks didn't reach them, at least they came close. The wake of the tugboat remained carved in marble. I put one of my three surfboards into my foreign, albeit second-hand, van. I put on dry clothes, ate a chocolate bar and drank a vitamin-enriched juice. I lit one up, threw half of it away. I called Rubén and, though we talked for a while, we didn't say much. Then I got upset and, before going home, vomited all over myself.

Twenty-seven
Sushi

The Japanese need raw fish. Their fishing fleet discovered years ago that the shoals were constantly moving farther away from the coasts, so they had to develop a system for bringing their catch to land.

What did they do?

They froze the fish. They organized groups of ships in which three or four large cargo ships would accompany a fishing vessel, ready and waiting to freeze the catch, and another was there to supply fuel. After all this, they realized that the ultra-frozen fish lost its fine flavor and the consumer would pass it up in favor of the fresh catch.

So, what did they do then?

They again modified the flotilla, adapting the large freezer ships by installing pools of salt water where they could store the fish alive and bring them to the coasts to sell at market. Now they had another problem. The fish arrived alive, yes, but not swishing their tails. To optimize the yield from the offshore fishing, the fish had been held in tanks aboard the ships. The haul arrived in port lethargic and rigid, which directly affected the texture, flavor and, most importantly, sales at market. The result was not satisfactory at all. So, now what did they do?

They brought together engineers, gluttons, bosses, fishermen, and restaurateurs. By the end of those long meetings, in which everyone was constantly checking their cellphones, they had only managed to agree that they had to keep the current infrastructure since the fleet had been renovated twice, and the investment had not been amortized, and what was most important was not just to keep the fish alive but to keep their tails swishing. The consistency and fleshiness had to be appropriate when transferring it, with paddles, from the trays of the wooden ships to the mouths of the consumers.

So, what could they do? Put them in an even larger pool on land and wait for them to recuperate from their lethargy? What to do, huh? What to do? Once again, the simple solution was innocent and sinister at the same time. To imitate nature is to overcome it, you could hear in the hallways during the snack breaks. They put a small shark in the pools on the cargo ships and let the food chain, natural selection, and instinct do the work as the great experts went out and chased transvestites through the night all around the convention center. A shark only eats out of hunger. The rest of the time it swims nervously around the pool, trying to find a way out, because there has to be a way out, somewhere. The thousands of fish in the tank swished about as they never had before, fleeing over and over again from the danger whose appetite, out of modesty, they never inquired about. Thus, the tuna bellies now arrive to port fortified and glossy.

Twenty-eight
Your House

You've started going away again. There's constantly more of you on the sheets and in my smile. A lethal gas floating in the atmosphere. I like you. I like you for me. Yesterday you cooked lasagna, you watered your lawn, and you glanced at me mischievously. Aches and pains blossomed for us in remote latitudes. I get dizzy all over again with you near me. I adore your pursed, circumspect mouth about to tell me some truth, reconsidering the best way to go.

Your awesome home, your hideaway home, your tricky home. The wood glows on the stairs and top floor. It smells of the countryside, the countryside in bloom. The mint planted beneath the kitchen window, in an old washbasin, rises to the sill and you can stand on a chair and stretch your arm out to reach it. The aroma wraps around your fingers until the following morning. The walls are still rough. The light enters through every window, all the time, without discriminating between sunrise and sunset, without a care for time. It's oriented towards the sun. You moved some things around, but the old fireplace, now closed, behind blackened glass, is still where it always was. You belong to the house. You form part of a succulent whole. With great care I remove the few clothes you still wear. When I drop your panties they get tangled at your ankles and I bend down to free them. With your legs overhead, bent at the knees, you bring your feet towards me; your eyes are wide open, containing a smile that will ultimately spill from your mouth. I pass my hands over your feet and you pull back with the slightest jolt your body has ever known. You have candles everywhere, on your books, in the bathroom, hanging from a metal blind that separates nothing from no one. I toss your panties behind me, I grasp a foot and massage it, I bring it toward my face, I lick its sole, holding it with both hands so it won't go running away with you behind it. While your skin decides whether you're ticklish, my melting eyes peruse your body from south to north. You put your toes in my mouth, carefully separating them with my tongue. I savor them as you open your mouth slightly and rub your face against the pillow. The house only has two doors, the entrance and the one that separates everything else from the bathroom. Scarcely a single lock. Honest and transparent as the dew that covers the house at dawn.

Twenty-nine
Bala-Bala

The people at the hotel are soft and gooey. And that's because, for anyone to finance a week here in the off season, they have to be sharks in their own right. They unsuccessfully try to hang themselves with their own Windsor double-or-nothing knotted ties, in the luxurious offices in the city's center. The tourists of high standing, in their polo shirts and white terry-cloth bath-robes, insist on windsurfing at the private beach. There's no sun, no wind, nor is it a propitious spot for doing such a thing. But here they have the opportunity to put on their new neoprene wetsuits, tense up their muscles, long atrophied in board meet-ings, and tan their skin a little in honor of Coco Chanel. From the way they take such extreme precautions, slathering on sun-block lotion, you can see they still believe dark skin is only for field hands.

Today I had breakfast at an incomparable all-you-can-eat buffet. I got up early so I could fully enjoy it. The hotel dining room was aglitter with water fountains whose lights kept chang-ing colors. A man was playing the harp marvelously. When I greeted him, he made a mistake in the piece he was perform-ing. He seemed more comfortable being invisible to the diners. I had to return to my room because the maître d' amiably showed me a sign inviting everyone to dine in harmony with the entire world and, for this reason, the sign strongly suggested we cover our sexualized thighs. In hotels like this one, no one expos-es their knees unless they have ulterior motives. I stayed here, stretched out and relaxed, thanks to an error by The Company, which hired me by mistake in the first place. At night I couldn't sleep, so I went out for a walk. It took me three beers to realize that I was engaged in an exhaustive search for the perfect kara-oke, inspired once again by his gracious majesty and seasoned by yet another world cup soccer tournament, which was now upon us. I discovered the disco all the other travelers had been talking about, extolling its class and air of British singles bar. La Saxo. At the mouth of the entrance, in flashing blue and white neon lights, was the announcement: Family Fun Disco. Karaoke and billiards open to the public, which in those days and at those hours was very scarce. On my way back to the hotel, I wandered into the Sir Arthur Pub. It astonishes me to see a disco pub with so much medieval decorative armor for tourists. A full set of armor with sword and inscription, Excalibur, engraved in gold, a shield embossed with a horde of lions along the top. That evening the clientele was deformed into a mythological creature, half sunburnt freckle-faced girl, half someone else's bigger-than-life butt, and then there was the sangria-intoxicated friend who, despite her efforts to embody the living symbol of Eurowhore, attracted hardly anyone's attention as she sipped from her wineglass. They both possessed the visual abilities of chameleons, aware of any and all movements by those who were potential predators or prey. They acted like go-go girls, inaccessible and divine. Supraterrestrial haughty Go-Gophers. Supply and Demand, hand in hand. Surrounded by the local studs, dressed in weekend finery, lined up like turtles. Second-generation Maghrebians, assimilated and wearing lots of cologne and selling 20-euro packets of something they insist is really good shit. Some uniformed hooligan and about twenty bored waiters doing their best for another night to be so fuckin' funky despite the impossible challenge presented by the Latino Cabrón Cuatro anthology playing in shuffle mode.

THIRTY
GECKO

We had a pet. We found it in your storage room while we were cleaning. It jumped out from all the rusty cans and then it was black, like the darkness that sheltered it. It fell into my hands, startling me, then he was frightened and jumped back on top of the cans. I cornered him and, to be honest, spoke to him in a sweet, gentle way as if he were a cat. After chasing him around dried up old paint cans, damp rags that had been there for years, and crusted tools, I put him in a glass jar, empty of marmalade. He was my prisoner. I screwed the top on, perforated with pin holes so he wouldn't die. He was pretty: covered with scales, dark brown, like a broken branch in the rainforest, and his protuberances were green like the color of the sea. We continued to empty out the storage room. Every now and then I'd check on him. He was so pale I began to worry. Perhaps he was suffocating, perhaps holding his breath to put an end to his captivity. A little later I came to understand his mimetic nature. He was assuming the light brown color of the unvarnished fruit box that sat beside him. A nice lizard, with changing colors, fat fingers because of his suction cups, and a belly that was always in contact with the ground. We would let him run freely up the walls of your house so he could serve himself to the insects he caught near the lightbulbs. It took us a while to discover his name, although it came to us after the third glass of wine at dinner.

THIRTY-ONE
THE PUDDLE

Paradise is also called the Puddle, and Club No One. It's not even a beach. Volcanic phlegm that the crater once spat out in a rage all the way to the sea. The bastard completely covered The Island with its smegma, molding it to its liking. Black, porous rock spewed along the shore and an atoll that, in theory, protects against the breaking waves. The lava and the dark rock are gently kept moist by the rising and falling of the tide. In its most remote corners, together with the smallest puddles, which are only refreshed when the water strikes with full force against Paradise, you can see traces of salt-like sips already taken from a beer served with a generous head. At Club No One, there are two rules: it's nudist for nudists, and the only tip permitted is painted in white irregular letters on one of the large black rocks that guard the path: "Pick up your leftover food." You know you're getting close to the Club when the path is no longer red dirt, lined by shrubs rustling with bluebeards among the branches and rocky crags. During the descent to the shore, the lizards can be seen sunning themselves at noon or fleeing through the rustling dry grass. The rocks, those that form part of the livable parts of The Island, those that were not upchucked by the volcano, lie in enormous fragmented formations, aligned by the rains. The rockslides during the rainy season transform the access path into a labyrinth of obstacles. You have to walk through the split center of a rock, several meters tall, that fell across the path so as not to fall into the sea, stepping over crunching gravel. So, Paradise changes as a function of Autumn's forces. There is yet another rule, not written on any rock. Once people have put their clothes back on, and picked up their leftovers and fruit rinds, and thrown them into the sea, and started climbing the gigantic steps of dried and deformed lava toward the reality that lies at the other end of the path, after winding through the slabs of The Island that have toppled over from the rains, they bid Paradise farewell. And they say goodbye to one another. It's not a question of neighborhood manners, nor because you might need someone's help at any moment, like in the mountains. The people who go to this place are accomplices, and at the same time, keepers of a secret, and when they say goodbye with a simple smile or a gentle wave of the hand, they are conspiring to never reveal the location of Paradise. You can get there by walking. It is rarely empty. There are almost always people there. Two, three, seven people. But the rocks form asymmetric terraces at different heights, and the sun takes care of warming them during the day. The breaking waves send cold water, in agreeable gusts of spray, up to and over the members of Club No One. From one terrace to another there are impassable distances, albeit in inches, so no one bothers anyone. Yesterday, we were practically alone. Behind one of the black lava peaks we occasionally saw a couple of heads bobbing up and down. Later, a girl came along whistling an original melody. She whistled well for a French girl. She undressed and immediately went swimming in the big pool where the water constantly washes in and out after crashing on the ledges and the bottom is often an unbelievable green. She bathed, then sat by the shore. She had adorable large, calm, soft, breasts. Her nipples: the finishing touch on the magnificent fabric of her body. She stood up and whistled a new stanza to her melody. She stopped whistling and dove into the water. We were smoking and talking and embracing to protect ourselves from the chill wind. The woman wrapped an orange beach towel around her waist and began to transcribe the melody she'd been whistling onto blank sheet music.

We went there again the day before yesterday. The weather was nicer. It was around noon, we'd been in your house, making slow love, as soon as we opened our eyes. We made a stop at the bar with the best squid on The Island, and we ordered food to take to Paradise. It came with salad, fried potatoes, lemon and house-made alioli. You brought a cooler with beer and chocolates. A perfect plan. When we arrived at the Puddle, no one was there. All the terraces were deserted. The sea was angrily beating the shore. Something was bothering it. The sun invited us to swim, but the water was discouraging. I took off my clothes, you didn't. When all the beer was gone, you lay face down and were soon fast asleep. The stones contributed to the warm glow of your skin, delicately covered by a few minuscule threads of fabric. I watched you and we lay side by side for a long time. I carefully touched you without interrupting your rest. Rather than pounce on you, I took up my Log and reluctantly leafed through it. Between paragraph breaks I gazed, sideways, at your butt, my tongue involuntarily and slowly running along my upper lip. Then it crept up your back, hopping from vertebra to vertebra, always culminating at your smooth, resting face. Little by little, you began to awaken. Swollen eyes, your voice heavy. I ran my hand across your back, just above your bikini. You were smoldering. You were like sheer, hot metal. Your lips glistened and I couldn't help but caress you as you asked what I was writing in my Log. I kissed you, falling at your side, and I sent my fingers walking over your skin. We were the only ones in Paradise. Perhaps there was no one else on The Island. You embraced me, loosely, not quite ready to relinquish your contact with the rock. I smiled, exposing my elongating fangs, untying the upper knot, a fine thread that quickly fell away as my teeth calmly twisted and released, modestly. You opened your eyes, checking for witnesses. Meanwhile I sought your nipple between the rock and your body. We pressed together and you said slow. I didn't hear you because my hand was already untying the lower knot. Pulling on one of the laces I found your butt. Final, unappealable, indissoluble, unbreakable. There was a smooth tan line. I touched your ass, stroking it and gently resting my face against it. The aroma of your hidden recesses drove me crazy from the first time they were accessible. An organic fragrance and, though insipid, complete and ethereally perfumed. So much of you I could hardly tolerate it. I kissed your cheek and drew near to your infinity until I had it within reach of my tongue. I lost myself there with mouth open, eyes closed, as you twisted. You asked me what I was doing, or something like that. I stretched above you. I was steaming as I melted into your sun baked back. So often we laid this way in bed, talking quietly, one on top of the other. Sometimes changing position, still in a pile. I loved feeling your body on top of mine. And mine on top of yours. I slid upward, carefully, until finding the hollow formed by the two hemispheres at the base of your back where a sweet nectar was meandering. I completely collapsed, my body on top of your gasp; your breath vibrated through your lips, ready to be explored. I kissed everything within reach and passed my hands beneath your body, supporting the bones at your waist.

The sun burned down on the dry lava, the sea pounded Paradise, sending cool spray into the air.

"I have to have you." You squeezed your eyes shut and nodded your head, leaning your head forward enormous millimeters. You opened your legs slightly and immediately I entered. Radiant, you waited. You, too, were lava. I melted to the rhythms marked by the sun, the stone and the water, occasionally spraying our backs. We looked around us: our bodies had achieved such complete composure, we had no desire to share with others. We squirmed just enough to compete with the sun and cause it to hesitate. We were lizards peering into Paradise having wandered afar in search of ripened fruit. Tense, arching, in a sun-induced torpor, from time to time craning our vigilant necks. Thus we passed an entire lifetime moving one with another, struggling to fall to pieces, gathering the light of the sun, the breeze, and the salt that was now the only thing that reached us from the sea. We brought our mouths together in a kiss, writhing wildly.

We destroyed the instant and transformed it into the infinite, adorned in pearls of perspiration, I escaped the lava of your interior and released myself, partly on your back, partly into the stone bay. We moaned, keeping watch so that no one would share our fortune. We embraced powerfully, transforming the infinite back into the instant. We loved each other with glimmers of underwater topaz. We stared at one another, unable to speak. The sea went calm. It, too, we had tamed. We melted like snowflakes on the ground. We went into the water until we were wrinkled and covered by the crafty, starry, swaggering night.

Thirty-two
The Queen

Returning to Quemada Beach means seeing Chicho again. On The Island, it is not common for surfers to go from place to place. They don't go in search of waves, they wait for the waves to come to them on their own beaches. It doesn't matter if the waves take a week or a month. When the sea is good again, they walk down from their houses to the shore and this seems to give some of them the right to become chiefs of the spindrift. There are others of us who travel the necessary kilometers, and sometimes that means a lot, to reach a place like this one, where the roads dead end and are swallowed by the sea. Many of us are outsiders. *Godos*, tourists, *gringos*, strangers, immigrants, foreigners, with feet instead of roots. Many of us have no place of origin. When there are waves at Quemada Beach, the first thing you see on the peak is Chicho's board and his grey mane. It is not a thoroughfare beach, rather it is at one of the extremes of The Island, after which there is just more sea. If you go there, and Chicho's about, everything's okay. A one-hundred-fifteen-pound Neptune, a head of long hair and eyes that change color according to the state of the sea. To surf alongside Chicho is to see how energy passes through and modifies people. To see that we must pursue our dreams rather than be caught by them. To learn, to enjoy, to be cheered when you grab one. Now and then he stiffens and points like a hunting dog , he forgets everything else, he points his board to an odd place in the distance and, as if he had an appointment, paddles to his rendezvous with an amazing peak. There, Chicho and the wave kiss in desperation. Chicho flies and dives, fast and slow, inside and outside, and back deep inside. Chicho will mess with any wave that's worth the trouble. When that kid was carried away by the current, Chicho paddled hard after him, the way he'd been paddling after his lovers all afternoon. The rest of us, not knowing what to do, stayed where we were, waiting, and when someone finally decided to do something, Chicho was already coming back with the frightened kid in tow. He took him right up to the shore, pounded his back, then came back out to where we were to try to grab a few more rides. When he caught up to us, Chicho flashed us a toothy grin, his teeth worn down, discolored, but mostly intact.

"Shit, the Queen almost carried him away, he practically lost his Bermudas, the little bitch!"

"Who's the Queen?"

Chicho threw the hair back from his face, straddled his board so that his Bermudas slipped down and exposed a pale butt cheek, in contrast to his tanned back, smiling broadly and seeming to silently reminisce before telling us about her.

The force of the ocean in Indonesia is a demonstration of the full power of Nature. Its brute forces travel directly and without detours from Antarctica. Many have drowned there on remote beaches, especially to the south of Java. From generation to generation, these drownings have been attributed to the desire and whims of the Queen of the South Seas. Every year the spirits of this ocean tally up a significant number of young people, snatching them from the beaches and converting them into forced lovers in her lethal courtship. Tsunamis and entire shoals of dying fish, flopping on the sand as if they could still reach the water, have been attributed to Ratu Nyai Loro Kidul. To ward off more tragedies, every day on the nicest beaches offerings are laid out: bowls of braided flowers, incense, fruit, cigarettes, and sometimes paraffin. Then prayers are offered, beseeching her to be good. At the Hotel Samidra, in Palabuhan Rato (Harbor of the Queen), there is always a vacant room for the Queen, and no one else is allowed to stay there under any circumstances. This decision was made when a three-meter wave swept over the opening ceremonies for the hotel in 1966. A local shaman had warned of the tragedy several weeks earlier. If you don't make offerings first to the Queen, you shouldn't do anything. In 1991, the Grand Bali Beach Hotel had a fire that burned through 95 per cent of the rooms. Room 327 was the only room that was spared. It had been empty since the opening and was reserved for Ratu Myai Loro Kidul. Following its completion, the Grand Bali Beach Hotel has kept that room reserved for the Queen, and has even added all kinds of Asian luxuries. Ministers with their ceremonial sashes and stern faces make daily offerings in the gardens of the hotels, in doorways to shops and homes, at crossroads, on beaches, and in restaurant alleyways.

They say that when the Queen of the South Seas takes a liking to a young man, she tears off his Bermudas, which are found later on the atolls, or on the beaches, or near the lighthouse in Poris Bay. So, if the Queen only takes young men without clothing, what better protection could there be than to wear shorts under your swimsuit?

THIRTY-THREE
DAY OFF

I only realized when I got out of my van. Shit, I thought, out loud. I forgot it. Shit, shit, a thousand times, shit. I accompanied the word by pounding on the hood. Shit, because I knew exactly where I forgot it and when I no longer had it with me. Shit, because it wasn't mine and, aware that there are two kinds of idiots—those who lend books and those who return them—I tended to belong to the second group. Shit, because the book had me confined, breathing it as if I were at a banquet of continuous flow air. Shit, because it was a gift I gave you with the healthy intention of reading it myself, while respecting the rules of private property, of course. And even more, shit, because in appreciation of my attention to detail and the fantastic content of the book, the order of its words, and the scrupulous chaos of its concepts, you had come up with a perfect tool, a paper compass to avoid becoming lost in its pages. I left it on the plane, after hours of working in that tube, serving beverages and peanuts, practicing the choreography of emergency exits, seatbelts, oxygen masks, and life vests. After serving tomato juice garnished with lemon slices delicately handled with metal tongs, I returned home by plane, but this time as a passenger. My companions were sleeping as a consequence of oxygen deficiency, the peace that comes with knowing your workday is over, and the certainty that you don't have to keep smiling into empty space. For my part, I had drunk too many staff coffees with two sugars and a splash of milk. The caffeine still distracted me. I opened the book, feeling calm. I was no longer at the beck and call of the passengers asking for water or looking for the bathroom. And there, again, was Osita, the Little Bear, and El Lobo, the Wolf, braving their adventures astride the Red Dragon. I felt everything that happened to them very deeply. The text was accompanied by photos, drawings, and notes written on a typewriter. At times, beginning a new paragraph, I would go back a few pages and look once again at the smiling faces, and study what they were wearing, or what bottle of wine they had on their fold-out tables. I traveled many miles with them and they made a space for me on Fafner, their Red Dragon, who sometimes disguised himself as a Volkswagen. When we landed, according to protocol, I had to keep my Company ID card where it could be seen. I'm supposed to wait until the tube is empty of all passengers, their Bermudas, and briefcases. I have to say goodbye to the technical crew, thank them for carrying us, even though I had a paid ticket on that flight, then I can grab my bag, say goodbye to my workmates as they're leaving the plane, and thank them for serving me juice during the flight, greet the new crew as they enter, get my book, and go home.

I got distracted. Probably while waiting for the line of passengers in the aisle to disembark. I was following a woman's legs along the passageway toward the exit. They weren't necessarily that pretty, but they were the legs of a woman. The decompression began in the same moment that the sun's rays hit my forehead for the first time in what seemed like an eternity of being in a metallic tank. Leaving the airport I inhaled reality, plants and cars. The air smelled of relative humidity, of stew in a nearby house, of eucalyptus in the park on the other side of the highway, of garbage recently dumped somewhere off in the distance, and of summer perspiration. Ahead of me: three whole days off. I could feel the expansion of internal gases, the fruit of submitting a body like mine to a stagnant, foul, and pressurized environment for so many straight hours. I put on my sunglasses and headed towards the parking lot, not feeling any hurry. Straight to the beach to see if there were any waves, and that night maybe get drunk. Then we'd sleep until we got tired of sleeping. Shit, shit and more shit. Kicking the mudguard of my van sprained my foot and gave me a skin rash. How could I forget something

76

like that? I was a disgusting Iscariot. I put a rescue plan into motion. It was desperate and abundant in vagueness, but I had no other. I called my workmates, the ones I had just seen boarding the plane, who were beginning their journey as I ended mine. All their cell phones were turned off. That meant the plane was probably in the air. A bad situation. The cleaning service had probably swept through like a plague of termites, as demanded by the Company during the brief stopovers. If they had come through, there were three possibilities: one, that they found the book and, unless someone told them not to, they would have thrown it into a huge black garbage bag, together with sick bags covered in chewing gum, empty cans, plastic cups, and napkins bearing the crimson Company logo; two, that they hadn't found it and it was now flying to some remote destination; and, three, even less likely, that someone had found and kept it. In this case, the person would have had to take a few minutes to dive into the first paragraphs and to discover a plot buried in the words, or to simply surrender to them, as I did. The incomprehensible title—unless you immediately grasped the rules of the simple play on words—and the photograph on the cover of a lanky, bearded man—the author—with a strange expression and posture, holding a white and orange striped traffic cone as if it were a hat, all invited the reader to peruse the pages inside, or, perhaps, to toss them delicately into a black plastic garbage bag. It was not thick, didn't look like a bestseller, definitely not *The Da Vinci Code*. The next thing I did was to get undressed and then it sunk in: I had a few days completely free. I would take a shower and leave behind me the complacent, woody, virile, mature and sensitive fragrance I conceded with absurd courtesy to the passengers as I leaned over them to hand them beverages or to turn on their reading lights, hundreds of times, day after day. Half naked, I searched the house for the list of phone numbers of my co-workers. I took off my nylon socks and threw them out the window. I chose a few names and numbers of people

77

who, perhaps, might be on the same plane as the book. I tried to compose a text message that would motivate, inspire and mobilize whoever might read about my impending disaster. With the finite number of characters determined by a text message, I sent it out to three different numbers and I also left a message in their voice mails begging them, in case they heard this message in time, to look for, find, and safely put away, the object of my desire, which wasn't even mine.

You were surprised that I would give you such a book, with its disconcerting cover, and excess of creativity and plot in which the main characters take thirty-three days to travel from Paris to Marseilles. By the fact that I gave it to you in Epicentro, where we had agreed to meet to get as much as we could from each other in such monstrously few hours. By the fact that when I gave it to you, with some other trinket, my eyes waited for a few seconds to catch the reaction in your eyes, and then shifted to rest on those thick, succulently appealing pages.

The book and I already knew each other, although we hadn't become intimately acquainted. Feli used to stop by with it. He would always put it on the seat next to him in the waiting rooms of airports and train stations. Feli's edition of *Autonauts* had a special quality of never losing its aspect of purity. The white cover of the pocket edition always conserved its color, always shiny although it had been on platforms, coasts, and terminals. It never got dirty, nor did it get splattered by the contents of open cans of drinks or marinated mussels that Feli would handle with the same hand as he handled the book. He'd gotten it as a gift, from someone who assumed he would have a kind of affinity with it. He had a van, much more modern that Fafner, although it had the same Westfalia roof bed, which made it seem all the more like a dragon. But Feli didn't seem to read very much. His book had no signs of wear, no dog ears where he had stopped reading, no notes in the margins, no bookmarks. A virgin, he carried it with him at all times. I once saw another edition in the house of a friend, a sufficiently close friend to consider borrowing it because she would never have noticed it was missing. I skimmed a few paragraphs at random on a night we went to the girl's family home in the mountains. A house and storage space in which old furniture sits, half dead, among used books from the main house and a black-and-white television no one dares throw out because it still works. The reason for our trip was a double date with a friend of my friend and someone she had once slept with, and she was hoping for a repeat. I soon discovered that it was my friend who had an almost certain plan with the other guy. So, as it turned out, it was up to me to try to seduce someone I'd never met but with whom I would not have minded spending the night in bed. For that to happen I would have had to be willing to worship her from the portable altar she brought with her, at least on that night, and I suppose every time she left her home. I was having an iconoclastic night, which is why I was determined to poison myself, to observe, and to launch explosive objects at the girl from my mouth. I don't know if the three of them ended up in the same bed. I know that after that my friend no longer called me with the same frequency as before. For me, there was only one way to combat tedium, and that came in the form of a girl with pearl earrings who only spoke in the very first person singular. I conducted an exhaustive search of the house's library, looking for a jewel. They had a good selection of contemporary books and three seminal books from our parents' day, now relegated to their country home. *Escape From Freedom* (Fromm), *Steppenwolf* (Hesse), *One Hundred Years of Solitude* (García Márquez), *Datebook of the Optimistic Woman 1971* (Telva magazine), and, finally, there it was again: *Autonauts of the Cosmoroute* (Cortázar and Dunlop). I closed myself up in the bathroom and leafed through all of them. *Autonauts* had a three-sentence, handwritten-in-black-ink dedication that promised a great travel book. I wasn't impressed. What was delivered was a book with all the pages marked by comments and underlined sentences. Question marks and exclamation points everywhere. Someone had really worked it over. I set all the others aside immediately. Then, before someone insisted that I come out of the bathroom, since it was too cold to go outside to pee, I read almost a hundred pages of which all I remember is having a terrible urge to travel over land, along the asphalt scars of France. As a souvenir, I took the *Telva* datebook with me, partly because it felt like committing a misdemeanor—not a crime—and partly because it contained a priceless collection of photographs of liberated and independent women, resolved and hardworking, who, despite occupying positions of responsibility, having flourishing families, and maintaining their emotional lives, were always perfect, confidently setting fashion trends year after year.

I went on vacation and was able to forget about everything, except Fafner, the Little Bear, and the Wolf. I also began to forget about ever getting them back. My text messages, bottles tossed into the sea, pleas for help, had all gone unanswered. The book was probably forgotten among piles of newspapers and magazines, gathered up by the cleaning service, or buried beneath mounds of organic residuals in an inland dump somewhere, with seagulls circling overhead. Back at work again, I checked my mailbox with fingers crossed, only to find that the book wasn't there. I then interrogated my workmates. It seems that a couple of them had followed its fate, without much interest, after they'd received my desperate messages. They were sure they'd seen it around for a few minutes. But they weren't sure where, or for how long. They didn't even know what the book looked like. I was barking up the wrong tree. One woman recommended that I check with the operations office, the other woman thought it would be better to ask at the main office. One thought the other woman had sent the book to one of those offices, and the other woman thought I was just trying to get a date with the first by creating this elaborate and lame excuse, albeit innovative. I didn't want to go home empty-handed and have to admit to its owner that I'd forever lost her book. Mustering forces for that fateful moment, after such a long day, my last hope was to go to the biggest bookstore on The Island, pray that they would have a copy on their shelves, and try to buy it. Then I would perform the laborious task of making it look old, including dog-earing the pages that, because of their special interest, had been marked in the original, and putting asterisks over the words that had caught your attention. To this end, I was depending on the implement you had given me as a guide, which were four pages in twelve-point sans-serif font, and a CD. On the cover of the CD was a photo of you posing the same way as Cortázar holding his book. In cutoff blue jeans, black socks, white sneakers, in the sunny outdoors, and with a traffic cone on your head (which you stole for the photograph but carefully returned later to the recently paved highway from where you grabbed it, taking the same precautions in both phases of the operation). And, of course, shirtless. You had the same staged stance as the author in the photograph, but that wasn't enough for the two luscious fruits on your chest to go unnoticed, bare and brilliant, taunting the camera and whoever dared gaze at them. I never found out who took that photo of you. Behind the cover: three typed pages with the previously mentioned annotations from the book, and the CD, with all the musical references. Thanks to you, and to Carol (the Little Bear and coauthor of the book, and fundamental travel companion), to Julio and to the book, I was thus able to hear Lutoslavski and his thirteen instruments, Susana Rinaldi, Jelly Roll Morton, and Fats Waller, as well as others I already knew. The dictionary held the meaning of the terms that had disrupted your reading.

Bathyscaphe: a kind of submersible vessel designed to resist high pressure and intended for the exploration of the depths of the sea.

It also had many culinary and gastronomic terms.

Peas: *Guisantes*

Artichokes: *alcachofas, soplones, delatores.*

You also added some of your own succulent contributions, such as:

Cronopio: word invented by the author (referring to unconventional human beings).

Fendant: An appellation from the French winemaking region, or a well-known and prestigious vineyard (I'm not sure).

Coccinella: A coleopterous insect that is trimerous, very small, has a hemispheric body with black spikes (that is, a ladybug!)

Passing near a counter I had never thought much about and had no idea what it was for, I heard two angry passengers reporting a lost suitcase, and I realized it was the airport lost and found. I had no illusions, nor the strength to summon any, but that's where I went.

"Listen. I lost a book the other day on an airplane and I've looked for it everywhere. And to tell you the truth, I already…"

The lady, or young lady, who didn't even deign to look at me, interrupted and asked me: "Name?"

"Mine? Eric, I mean Stevenson, no, no, Chicho."

"Not your name, the name of the book!"

"Oh, *Autonauts of the Cosmoroute.* It's white and, I don't know, very inconsistent, although it's still a great travelogue."

"A what? Okay, listen, here's your stupid book. Now, leave me alone!"

The young lady, or not so young, handed me the book, and when she turned back to her photos of Ana Obregón in a swimsuit in the pages of her magazine, I leaned over the counter and kissed her on the lips.

"Look what I've brought!" I barged in and devoured you, with the book in hand, to somehow dilute my confession. I lifted you onto the kitchen table and licked your throat as you gently squirmed. I pulled off your apron, which held an aroma of arugula, and slid the straps of your sleeveless T-shirt from your shoulders with my teeth. Before settling on top of me, you pulled the shades of the windows. In this sense, yes, you were a bit miserly in not sharing the rays of light that radiated from our bodies as they did battle. I took up the book again where I had left off, calmly turning past the previous pages. Something had happened to it. It wasn't the same. To begin with, the dedication was in French, or at least that's what I thought. Upon closer inspection, it turned out to be a textual quotation, protected by parentheses, from page 315. "Damned be whoever thinks evil." Even the menus of the journey were a little different. Now, for many of their breakfasts, they drank passion fruit juice. But, how could that be? Passion fruit only grows in a few places in the world, such as your garden, and it's only called *parchita* in private. The scientific name is *passiflora caerulea*, although you always called it *parchita*. It has a strange flavor, which you eventually get used to only if it is prepared for you for several consecutive days. It's strong and sour and you have to dilute it with water. Cut a hole in the hard skin and empty it of its nectar, using a spoon to hold back the thousands of seeds, then mix it with condensed milk and add water or ice to taste. You can also add an orange, a banana, or an apple, and then strain it. All this is too inconvenient to do while traveling in a van. Then there were the descriptions of the rest stops. These were vividly described. So vividly you could see the tiles, feel the coolness of the morning on a Saturday, May 29, at 7:15 am. I could clearly hear all the noise around them, and there, between sounds of truck chassis and an early morning bird, came your own unmistakable, just arisen, footsteps on the gravel. Each chapter was unique, particularly the Pocket Guide to Lobos. In one excerpt, from page 330 and beyond, I found descriptions that fit me completely. "If you tickle him, he laughs wholeheartedly," "El Lobo has a confirmed tendency to dance in the woods, especially when there are stars," and "He is frequently seen in the company of a dragon." Skeptics will say that it's no more than a coincidence, that many of us could be wolves. But every time I reread these pages I find something even more disconcerting. The last time I dared open the book, the Guide to Lobos affirmed: "By his lazy nature, he has a chest full of hair, by his age, he seems irreconcilable with the interests you might suppose him to have, much of his hair has turned white, but on both sides of his Adam's apple he has some inconvenient hair that is more wolf-like than the rest, which he pulls with tweezers, to keep it neat and on its respective sides." My hair stood on end. The hairs on my chest, the white hairs, and even the inconvenient ones that always grow back on both sides of my throat.

I've lost other books on planes, several pairs of glasses and I never got anything back. Now I was reading the book constantly. As soon as I finished it, I would stare at the cover and begin to read it all over again, and when I was falling asleep, because the words now ran together in a familiar way, I would suddenly see a new sentence that had never been there before. Or a margin note that wasn't in my handwriting, or yours, referring to an album or a book I'd never heard of, and then, excited, I would go into the city and doggedly find it. Always references I would be delighted to find. Always with copyrights after '82, the year in which the book was written. A stifling night, returning to a page I'd read many times, bewildered, and which had affected me perhaps forever, I found it shaded by an eggplant-colored pencil. And that is the color of the paragraph that follows: "And little by little, if indeed writing is such an erotic experience as the two of us have always known it to be, we have to begin to open the doors of this book. To decide to emerge from this hesitation. Writing is always accepting the risk of saying everything, even, and above all, without knowing it." Lately some purple, sometimes green mold has begun to grow on the spine of the book, which, rather than destroying the cardboard of the cover, has been feeding it. On my night table I have a special edition.

I'm still delighted to find, for example, among the photographs, one day, a horrible figure of the Buddha, which was also on the television stand in my grandmother's house for as long as I can remember, and which she always said she'd found on the ground at a gas station, on the way to Marseille.

THIRTY-FOUR
OASIS

He's gone. One beautiful day he left, without haste or parsimony. He, who arrived captive in a glass jar. Nico, the skink, for three or five weeks had wandered the walls of our room, revealing himself up close. But one day, when I opened the window, he left with the utmost elegance as I tried to air out your house, and he climbed a couple of meters up the wall, but this time on the outside. Just far enough so my hands couldn't reach him. There, he turned his head and stared at me. Geckos can smile and Nico smiled maliciously. He was good-looking. His stay in the house had done him well. Now that he'd put on some weight, he was a healthy green, he was ready to leave. He went toward the ravine and there he stayed because, at night, the siren song of two hundred forty sexy frogs is an Islamic paradise for lizards.

THIRTY-FIVE
WET BUTT

My face, seen from where I am, in the rear view mirror, is that of a batrachian. Smashed, angry, screwed up. With my hair flat around my face, with seaweed stuck to my body. Seeing myself in the rear view mirror is to take an astral walk, to separate myself from my body and observe myself with sorrow and rage.

In my van, yes, driving. Driving while wearing my wetsuit. It's a short 3/2 suit. In the water it's ridiculous but functional. In the van it's the costume of a harlequin at a funeral. The water is getting cold, my butt is getting the seat wet, the van smells of salt. It's nighttime, I'm barefoot, my feet are bleeding.

The drivers of the cars I pass can't see me, but seated in the puddle forming on my seat, I'm aware of their laughter through tinted windshields.

It won't take me long to get home. I'm grateful I carried my keys with me into the water, tied around my neck on a shoelace. I turn on the radio and when I turn up the volume, a spark shoots through me from my heart finger to my shoulder. I'm grounded.

Somebody stole my backpack on the beach. The work of sodomites. All they wanted was to be a pain in my ass, they weren't after booty. The backpack had a pair of flip-flops, a T-shirt, a pair of shorts, some wax. I saw them. The thing is, I saw them from the sea. Someone crouching on the rocks. By the time I realized what was going on it was too late. I shouted from the shallows and they waved. I cursed and saw their gleaming smiles. So, now I'm soaked and barefoot, with my wetsuit on, driving in my van, at night, pissed off about everything.

I know who it was, I would recognize that moron out of a million morons. Bleached blond, security-guard complexion, broken nose.

He's really getting to me.

Thirty-six
Drowning

Drowning is pretty easy. All it takes is a sharp blow from the sea and you gulp her solution. It makes no difference whether you're fishing, in a boat, or even know how to swim. If a wave bowls you over hard enough to transform you into the laundry in your washing machine, if in the process it yanks off your Bermudas, or if all this happens at once and in one swift blow, game over. You've been inoculated with The Fear. The sea is very classy and will not drown you with her own hands. She'll fill you with panic, paralyzing your lungs, so that it's you drowning yourself. I saw what happened to you, I watched from the water. You were getting curious about the waves, so I gave you a body-board and some flippers. You were doing great, but after about half an hour, after riding a big wave, you would paddle back towards the peak and start shouting, "It's not worth it!" It was late afternoon and the sun was setting fire to the pieces of litter people threw on the ground. I dropped into the water, which was warm and gentle, seeming to lack force. Now you were sitting on the sand of the shore, putting on your flippers and wetsuit. The waves were lackluster, but if you timed them well they had a bit of a wall, just right for a lazy afternoon. When I glanced back at the shore, you were just getting into the water, with your back turned, so I paddled off to lose myself in the surf. I looked back at you and the water now came up to your waist. I looked towards the soon-to-be-setting sun and I smiled, taking a deep breath. Everything was in its place. Returning my gaze toward you, you were still on the same stretch of beach, or at least that's how it seemed from my vantage point. You were making strange gestures with your arms, your head appearing and disappearing. I only glimpsed your board occasionally and you were trying to shout my name, but the salty brine that filled your mouth wouldn't let you. I paddled as fast as I could towards you and a wave washed over me, not very powerfully. I kept paddling. I was only about fifteen or twenty meters from shore, and you were splashing about half that distance from the sand. The tide was going out fast, like an offended cobra. Your bodyboard was nowhere in sight. With bloodshot eyes, between gulps of saltwater, you managed to sputter that the leash had come off. Your bodyboard was already near the shore, washing up over and over on the sand. We were very close to each other. The crashing of the waves made it difficult for us to hear. Now, almost united, just a few strokes apart, you insisted on bobbing up and down rhythmically with terror-filled eyes. I shouted at you so loudly and hoarsely that I couldn't understand how you couldn't hear me. On one of those self-inflicted duckings you surfaced saying "the bodyboard, the bodyboard." We were now less than two meters away from each other. You spoke again, between gulps of seawater, and managed to say "the flippers, the flippers." You were holding them firmly in your hand, very concerned about not losing them, not losing them. I yelled, get rid of them. You ignored me again and now I was at your side. The sun was slowly descending behind a cliff draped with boxwood roots and was going to miss the denouement. I felt much more heat inside my body than outside, even though the water's warmth was exhausting. I asked you to climb on top of me. The two of us on my board would reach the shore in no time and all of this would be over. The waves broke timidly over us, I didn't find them threatening. You climbed to my shoulders and I kept paddling. Once again, piled on top of each other. I could feel your chest filling with air, emptying quickly, erratically, clipped, unable to keep up with its own pace. We were safe and sound. One wave caught us with a little more force, although ineffectively breaking over us, so I kept paddling and speaking words chosen to calm you down a bit, always in an upbeat voice to calm myself also. Here we are sweetheart, nice and easy, it was a scare, that's all. We're almost there, everything's going to be okay. But then another wave crashed over us and I lost you. A wave that was even wimpier and weaker than the previous ones, but it swept you from my shoulders. I'd be exaggerating if I said that we reached the shore quickly, that I easily found my footing, that the sweltering heat didn't get worse every time a new wave broke, that you weren't struggling there without believing that you had a chance, that I didn't shout louder and louder, that you didn't smash your knee against the largest rock in the bay, covered with thallophytes, and when I looked again toward the shore, people hadn't gathered to help you, or to help us, you didn't lose the bottom part of your swimsuit in the struggle, that when you set your feet on the shifting sand of the shore it didn't seem like the most solid land to you, I didn't take a deep breath because I had no idea that this was ever going to happen, on your knees dressed only in your wetsuit, with the rescued flippers beside you, you didn't belch and expel an enormous spout of water as if it had exploded from a hose. A huge swimmer, with glistening skin, approached you when you were close to the shore and offered you his board so he could bring you out. I felt guilty again, the bane of the Judeo-Christian. Guilt, hell, perhaps purgatory, penitence. I thought of how awful it would be to return later that afternoon alone, with a common pine box in the passenger's seat. You had just covered yourself with a beach blanket and were curling up on a rock. You didn't want anyone to come near you. The proximity of a stupid death, as usual, had rendered you lovely and fragile. You stayed on the beach, allowing me to hold you tight. Night had fallen and we fell back into silence.

THIRTY-SEVEN
THALASSOTHERAPY

Neither thalassotherapy—which television has still not fully explained to me—nor allowing myself to be completely coated in melted chocolate by expert hands that haven't the least intention of licking it off, nor reiki, nor yoga up my-ass. Rather, what works best for me, over all, is destructotherapy. For as long as I can remember, what has both calmed and triggered me, is to break everything. When the day only goes from bad to worse, from the moment I first open my eyes, I destroy a house. It's pleasant and tiring, which is why I like it. I prefer to destroy alone, although sometimes Eric comes along with appropriate tools and cans of sardines, beer, tomatoes, bread and onion for lunch. I've destroyed a ton of things, as I remember. The only resistance has come from my parents' marriage, which they managed to destroy themselves, and the bullet-proof glass at a bank branch. When I was fourteen years old, one summer, we found an abandoned hotel. All day in the street, skateboards underfoot or in our hands, sometimes just sitting on them. Four, five, six kids, sweating hormones and grinding every surface we could find. One stupid afternoon on which we'd already been chased off several plazas, accused of vandalism, someone said they were going to raze the hotel that same week. They were going to build a shopping mall with a multiplex on the ruins. We had never been inside the hotel's cadaver, which people said was filled with ghosts, orgies and a pool that was good for skateboarding. Without knowing whether we'd find a court of awaiting nymphs, horrific ghosts, or a puddle of green water filled with frogs surrounded by deck chairs, we set out on motorbikes and bicycles. Time only allowed for us to discover the pool, a hole in the form of a kidney, with smooth walls painted an impermeable blue, a sprinkling of puddles, and several drainage grates we put to use.

The sun beat down on our shoulders, as we went about mopping up. It didn't take long, we were adolescents. In no time, we were rolling on our boards. Unimaginable curves without end that left us with our mouths open in pleasure and surprise, and then we would fall. Stevenson was not a skater, he didn't like doing anything, not even staying at home, so he'd come with us. When someone would crash into one of the slippery walls, Stevenson would laugh, waving his beer bottle and saying, screw you. He was super lanky and could sprain his ankle crossing a street, or standing on tiptoe to reach whatever his father had hid on the top shelves of the closets. We thought we could stay and live there forever. Once we stopped skating, the sweat on our skin turned cold and Stevenson took us inside the hotel where he had been snooping around. Empty, but intact, it was impressive. The metal shelves were still in the kitchen and there were holes where appliances once stood. Stevenson enjoyed playing host as he amiably led us through the rooms with his arm extended like a receptionist. Diaphanous bedrooms, deserted and seemingly endless hallways, a cafeteria and banquet hall. We went from one side to another with skateboards and dilated pupils. Then we discovered destructotherapy. Rubén was the first to shift into destruction mode. He had just recently moved. His bulging eyes, the way he slurred his words, and his face covered with acne, all worked against him, but he'd come determined to establish a place in our gang. He began with a high-pitched scream and smashed a hall mirror with a kick he'd learned from some after-dinner movie. One thing led to another. We did skateboard tricks in the bathrooms, on the counters, in the elevator shaft. Eventually the skateboards went from our feet to our hands and then the only thing we wanted was to leave no stone unturned but to break everything. Stevenson included, taking great care of his ankles, he yanked out water faucets, screaming all the while, possessed by Rock 'n Roll. Before we collapsed, exhausted, a silence fell over the hotel of the type that precedes an explosion. Amid the noise and the rubble, we slowly desisted in our destructotherapy, without fully understanding why. In the distance we could hear a fuzzy humming noise, and then, with increasing clarity, police sirens, and so we quickly fled the hotel. Rubén immediately got on his bicycle and did his best to carry a crippled Stevenson, yelling and twisting like a scorpion caught in a fire. Those who could fled on their motorbikes, the rest on skateboards. The neighbors, in their chalets near the hotel, embracing couples in bathrobes, pointed fingers at us.

The house I'm destroying now is quaint, nice, located in an isolated area. I've smashed the studs, the ceramics, and the fixtures in the bathroom and kitchen. I've lifted the floor tiles. I've knocked down three stone walls, a chimney and two concrete benches reinforced with rebar. Without a mask, gloves, or brace to protect my kidneys. Nothing. The wall, the sledgehammer, the god on duty this morning, and me. It's a big house but discreet, which I suppose to be abandoned. Every time I come back, the only tracks I find are my own from my last demolition. It feels good to know you're part of this process of material transformation. I don't create, although I destroy, and it gives me pleasure not knowing exactly where I stand in all of this.

Then we grew, it was inevitable. And the consequence—also inevitable—was that we were inoculated with rage. We believed a revolution was still possible, but more importantly, that it would be fun. We would go to demonstrations, carefully choosing the most contentious ones. Unauthorized demonstrations, counter-demonstrations, demo-party-strations. We never chanted slogans. We didn't jump up and down, we didn't let ourselves be caught up in the spirit of group solidarity. We remained quiet and serious. When Rubén stopped making faces, when he became deadpan serious, an ominous shadow closed over the event. We were prepared. That was the signal. The wisest of leaders, those who are now in consulting firms, tended to approach us because they assumed our silence was an indication of docility and self-sacrifice. By then it was too late, we had already begun to screw everything up. We wore bandanas over our faces, and ski masks, we brought out slingshots and we offered cocktails to the security forces, hurling them from distances that were more intimate than prudent. We threw rocks at the riot police and storefronts. We threw posts through plate glass windows, sometimes looting without any particular interest in value, to leave everything destroyed in our wake. We cut in front of cars, blocked traffic, set fire to dumpsters, ran from the humvees, and we had fun. It was a risky sport. We were pretty good. The screwed-up system was our great and sufficiently convincing excuse to continue our destructotherapy, compensating for our own shortcomings and all that. We stopped when Stevenson was arrested, tried and convicted, and confined to a wheelchair. The mass evictions of the *Piolet de Trotsky* was the high point of our sporting career. A mall filled with squatters where we spent some unforgettable moments, as well as some nights of which we only have vague memories. We blew up several trash bins with firecrackers recently brought by Rubén from the Valencian *fallas*. The cops tried to lay a trap for us. As the antiriot police weren't enough, they requested reinforcements, but by then we were semiprofessionals and were able to mess around with them for a while, we lured them out of their patrol cars by stoning the windshields. Confused and stewing in their own cold sweat, they were pelleted by stones from the rooftops surrounding the plaza we'd led them into. Stevenson tripped as usual. Later, after all the hearings, background checks, and pre-trial detention, we decided that perhaps we didn't really have political vocations. Destructotherapy, like psychoanalysis, requires long treatments to be effective.

I like to close my eyes so fast that the splinters don't leave me blind in one eye. I'm good at fucking things up. Every two or three days, when the world again seems to be hand-painted, when it manages to bring out the worst of what's inside me,

94

what I thought I'd kept hidden so well but which comes to the surface like a body that drowned days before, I return to the house to swing the sledgehammer here and there, to jump on a recently extirpated bidet, or to smash the glass of some windows which for years had remained so proudly intact.

Thirty-eight
Half a Liter

An attractive couple. Athletic, good-looking, both dark-skinned and always smiling. They used teeth whiteners. Whenever Feli had a new girlfriend, he wouldn't leave her side until they broke up, and this one's name was Sandra. They climbed down the rocks leading to The Sewer in flip-flops and swimsuits. Feli was trying to turn her into a surfer. It's always better to sleep with a practitioner rather than a surf widow. The widows on the beaches become very tanned and admire up close the bodies that enter the water, they have the faces of femmes fatales, and they always feel lonely as they wait on the beach for their boyfriends to get tired of chasing sticks. Their equipment included a backpack for their wetsuits, Feli's surfboard, a mini-malibu, and a dog with a short name, spelled "Ch." Ch happily ran a few meters ahead, chasing the frightened lizards into the tall grass beside the path. When they arrived, the dog stood tense and still, his curly mutt's fur rigid, his eyes wide as he growled at the wrecked car that had now been there on the beach for such a long time. Sandra was clumsily doing the warm-up exercises Feli was teaching her, slightly embarrassed. Then, playfully, he helped her zip up her wetsuit, which gave her body an admirable shapeliness. He took his own suit out of the backpack and a leash for Ch, which he put on the dog and tied to the pack. Ch immediately began to bark in even measures of four-four time, and he wouldn't stop. Sharp like a sea urchin spine in the ear.
On the beach, Aurora's smile stretched across her face as she discovered the sea for the first time. She was wearing white sweatpants, rolled up to her knees so she could wet her feet. Her legs were also white, a more urban complexion, and covered in mosquito bites, mosquitos avid for novelties and substitutes. Hypnotized, she watched the foam forming where she

would never go because it was too deep. She didn't know how to swim. She marveled at the morning, her arms akimbo, holding a half-liter can of San Miguel beer in one hand. As she returned to the towels, water wings and sand pails, she smiled, exposing her few gray pearl-like teeth. Little junkie, both Feli and Sandra thought at the same time. They looked at each other knowingly, then glanced at their belongings in a pile near Ch. Sandra, Feli's blond girlfriend for the season, was already slowly entering the water, using her board as support to ease herself more comfortably into the sea. Feli was still looking for four or five round rocks to weigh down the backpack when a gleeful, naked child ran past him, running so fervently that he sprayed black sand in Feli's face before he reached his mother and hugged her thighs. She ran her hand through his hair, taking a long sip from her beer and contemplating the horizon.

If they tried to rob their possessions, his car keys, two bananas and a bottle of mineral water, perhaps Feli would have time to get out of the water and catch the woman in sweatpants, or the boy.

THIRTY-NINE
STEAM

I liked to see you wearing the skirt that was so long, so sheer, and so ugly. So devoid of beauty. Old and worn out, it seemed to have been made for you with its print from another era. The way it covered your flagrant thighs made me nervous. I held you and swung you through the hotel room as if I were a good dance partner. I stroked the outside of your skirt, I crumpled it taking advantage of the bridge offered by your legs and touched you beneath, sensing the dampness of your underwear, suggestive to my fingers. We twirled around the table in the center of the room and also around the bed, but we would have ample time for the bed, so I led you to the divan. You knew very well where we were ultimately going, so you enjoyed discovering this place for the first time. I fell along the line marked by the upholstery of the psychoanalytic piece of furniture and then rose above you. Your skirt was now crumpled against my abdomen while the sweet heat of your body gripped me, without force but without pause. Only your panties and my belt were in the way. I threw them out the eighth-floor window. The sofa immediately conformed to our geographies as I lifted your skirt. I wanted to see how your navel trembled, so prone to panic attacks. Your skirt now up around your neck and you, your hands raised and your head hidden for an instant, trapped, tormented, resigned, restrained, undressed and amused, all at the same time. We embraced as we danced some more, without music, to the low notes emanating from our bodies. A blush assaulted your face and we suddenly realized that the armrests of the divan were pinching our legs. We almost didn't care. I protected your knees with my hands so they wouldn't get hurt. My fingers wailed a formal complaint as they were crushed. Hearing them wail, you understood that I'd lost the use of my hands and you began to caress me with malevolence. You sought my nipples among the hairs of my chest, and you found them. You squeezed them and pressed your tense, open hand over them, then brought your mouth to them and together we stretched, arching, so that the divan gave way for a moment. Tangled up with each other, we crawled to the bed and unmade it, diligently, for the next couple of hours. In the shower we collaborated in reaching the most delicious corners of our territories. The soap bubbles flowed, everything had the fragrance of oats and the water was so hot it flushed our skin. It was a potent hotel shower that didn't let up, in contrast to our legs. We spent a long time fondling the sheen of our excessively clean bodies. Happiness was found, that afternoon, beneath the hotel showerhead, so steady we didn't have to close our eyes to protect them from the soap. We stared at each other like sorcerers practicing voodoo. I raised my head and felt the scalding water slide off my head. When I lowered my gaze again, you were gone. But you were still there, just lower down, on your knees, in front of me, your eyes half-closed, piercing me with tiny needles. You kissed me and pulled me towards you with your hands. With devastating delicacy you put my pleasantly slumbering cock in your mouth. You woke it up in no time. Relieved, I knew that they were made for each other, perfectly joined. My anatomy, so inscrutable and dubious, now made sense, after so many years. You stood up and transferred its flavor to my mouth, then you turned around, pressing your hands against the tiles of the shower and raised one of your legs, placing your foot on the edge of the tub. I entered you, resolute, and we sprayed the entire bathroom for an instant. I was lost in the immense galaxy that exists in one of the black holes of my brain. When I returned, the water was scorching my back. I held myself upright by grabbing hold of the shower curtain, almost piercing it with my fingernails. One of your hands appeared on the other side of the curtain and turned off the tap. The water stopped falling in the shower and sand ran again in the clocks.

You already had a towel wrapped around your body and as you arranged your hair you observed, defiantly, your image in the mirror fogged over by steam.

FORTY
MORE NEVER

Just out of the water, and before leaving La Quemada on my way home, I stopped in to see Chicho for a moment. The door was open, the padlock was hanging loose. I called him a couple of times but he didn't answer. The house was in its usual state of rigorous disorder, although it smelled more than ever of pot. I walked through the shack and reached the gate that opened onto the patio where three surfboards and two wetsuits were coquettishly drying under the electric blue sky. The faint sounds of a trumpet and trombone led me to Chicho. Squatting, shirtless, his back peeling and wearing an enormous straw hat, I thought he was naked. He had on a ragged pair of running shorts and was intently manicuring his plants.

"What's going on, Chicho?"

He jerked upright, turned, pointlessly protecting his fully mature plantation with his slight body.

"Shit! You scared me. How goes it, boss?"

"Fine, fine." I was doing well. I was coming from wooing the beach and the beach had been good to me.

"What are you doing?" I asked, though it was obvious.

"Nothing, just getting these little witches ready to harvest tomorrow." Chicho carefully placed the leaves he had just cut—with the utmost delicacy—from the main stem into a cardboard box. Half of the plants were now ready, without a single extra, useless leaf left on them, just burgeoning sticky buds with amber tendrils.

"Stick around and give me a hand. Man, I outdid myself this year. Twenty-eight plants and they're all bigger than I am. I might be getting too old for this, but don't kid yourself, I could smoke 'em all myself. The year is long, but it's getting to be too much work for me. More never!

"Hey, what time is it?"

He shrugged his shoulders, and so did I. When you ride waves a rupture in the Space-Time continuum takes place. Time, as we know it, evaporates, it transpires differently, in other measures, in which what is short becomes long and what is long becomes polished crystal submerged in mud. As for Space, a perpetual loop is formed, a compulsive and perpetual sequence. You paddle to point A (the peak) in order to reach point B (where the wave ends, you fall, or the wave closes out). This voyage is repeated over and over again. The spatial transition is the end in and of itself. No one tries to arrive at a destination, but rather to travel, over and over, the same trajectory, which is different every time. No two waves are ever the same, every wave is different. Even you are not the same as before you caught the last wave.

So, I stayed to help manicure, to complete the harvest, and to listen to Chicho. He lowered the volume, softening the sound of Alton Ellis trapped inside the radio, and told me, once again, two of his favorite stories, and confirmed that this was the perfect moment for the harvest.

FORTY-ONE
CHICHO SAYS

The retired men would get up early and walk with their metal detectors, collecting, much to their disappointment, tabs from soda pop cans. The women, those who had not been widowed, gathered in groups and walked, very quickly, in tight-fitting synthetic athletic wear. The snack bars were being sprayed down to remove the sticky layer of sangria on the floor, shrimp heads, and napkins from the night before when, then and there, casting a shadow over the yellow sand, came the invasion of desert scorpions.

What they were doing there was a mystery. Stevenson's father suffered from premature delirium tremens which often presented, out of the blue, before noon. Just as on D-day, at H-hour, in damp gray Normandy, the sand suddenly grew dark from the passage of hundreds of thousands of scorpions appearing out of nowhere. They lifted their tails, presenting them with the exhibitionism of a military parade. The beach was no more filled than usual, in early June the sky was dense, milky gray. Stevenson's father knew the next symptom would be a stinging sensation slithering over his skin, and then convulsions, tremors, nausea and almost certain death. A silly death, shirtless, with the shoulders and cheeks aflame, with a jar of after-sun lotion, seal still intact, sitting on the towel together with a can of beer. It wasn't exactly the type of death he'd imagined, but his funeral would have an exotic touch, back in Birmingham.

The authorities concerned did their best to maintain Playa Tullida as a fine tourist attraction when tourism on The Island was in decline. A beach near the capital, man-made and inoffensive, but judged according to the enormous terrarium it had become, no one would refer to it in such a way.

Playa Tullida had been a constant source of political conflict, fraud, and bribery in which every representative of the ruling class had participated to the best of their ability. Thus they had achieved the disconcerting grandiloquence of constructing this urban project. First, by constructing an enormous dam to protect the beach from the rare and unique lashings by the sea on the northeast coast of The Island, thereby creating a pretty and immense saltwater reservoir. Then the housing complex, including a horrific parking lot capable of hosting two thirds of all the motor vehicles on The Island on any given beautiful Sunday at the peak of the season. The cement block huts were sold at impossible prices and strictly through under-the-table deals, so that the titleholder would benefit from bulk sales of soda, wine and paella. To top it off, a shuttle system kept the beach well-supplied with towels and fresh tortillas every ten minutes. Its guts overflowed with Bermuda shorts, sleeveless white Ts, sandals, rayban sunglasses, and beach umbrellas in their primeval plastic sleeves, all poured into the bay. Chicho immediately explained it through conspiranoia. For Chicho, the evidence adhered as closely to reality as the swimsuits clung to the bodies of the girls, but he twisted it at his own convenience. Some holding company wanted the Playa Tullida concept to fail and for the tourists to be immediately redirected to other snack bars. The final explanation turned out to be just as scientific as it was unreal. On these islands they don't have what is called white sand, which in reality is essentially yellow sand, or, in the best of cases, sand-colored sand. So, following the principles of chromotherapy, to create an oasis of summery peace, it is necessary for the sand to be pure white.

The powers that be realized that just across the water, on the dark continent, they could get white sand and, consequently, they set to work. They bought an inordinate amount of cubic meters, out of fear that they wouldn't have enough, extracting it from the desert itself. The shovels of the excavators carried the sand, containing scorpion larva and all kinds of other microorganisms that were living their peaceful lives in the desert. The heat and the course of life took care of the rest. Now, in the collective imagination, the creatures scuttle around leaving white sand in the open picnic baskets containing leftover tortillas. Panicked crowds cause the access ways to collapse, the sun cracks the stones, the pickpockets take advantage of the situation and the scorpions would also flee from their cruel fate, if only they knew in which direction to run. But all of this is nothing more than a legend that can never be proven. Nonetheless, everyone who detests Playa Tullida loves to tell the legend over and over until they actually and fully believe it. Stevenson's father, given the least opportunity, will retell it, providing details that change with every version, so he can boast about how he defied death, whereas Chicho believes it even though he knows it can't be true, because human stupidity is twisted and knows no limits.

"Okay, but the thing about the Nazis, that certainly is true." Chicho shows me a collection of yellowed newspaper clippings, proving the veracity of the story. Ever since the First World War the Germans viewed The Island as an important strategic location. It goes without saying that the agreeable climate compared with freezing central Europe only galvanized that view. During the war the Nazi Academy of Science, the Ahnenenrbe, created by Himmler, was fascinated by the prehistory of The Island. They knew that early chroniclers mentioned a white race, blond and blue-eyed, tall and strong, with beautiful women. The academy promptly suspected that these were the first dwellers of Atlantis, in which they could clearly find features of the primitive Aryan race. "The formation of the head, the length of the arms and legs, and the skeletons of all the mommies on The Island, recall the formation of German bodies," according to Von Loeher. "And whoever doesn't accept that doesn't have a historian nearby." Chicho bursts out in laughter that turns into a bronchial coughing fit. The Nazi academy then thought of the Vandals, the Germanic peoples who were good navigators and settled in North Africa during the Roman Empire. They believed they could populate The Island after fleeing the Romans. The Nazis lost no time in sending their first expedition of learned scientists, setting up, as a front, the School of Island Archeology, whose specialty was undoubtedly craniometry.

"So, those idiots claiming the beaches as their own, covering it with their garbage, all pale and frustrated, if you do a little research it turns out they're more German than aspirin, you know?"

FORTY-TWO
SO, HERE YOU ARE

Aurora piled up rocks of different sizes, one on top of the other, in the same way as she piled up her failures. Large, cratered, small, and sharp. They followed no order of form or size. Instead, they seemed to be chronologically ordered. So, the balance of the tower was doomed, constructed on a base dominated by pebbles and high above were large rocks. She meditated, in communion with nature. She had learned to strip the sumptuousness from the grandiosity of simple things. She had been taught about Zen rocks at the day center. She had also learned to do patchwork, but that was an inadequate metaphor. Once in a while, she preferred to pile things, sometimes according to size, or the roughness of the rocks, their defects. She would return home the next day. The Sewer was almost vacant now, and the orange shades of the cloud wisps were causing her to dawdle before leaving. She was completing her sculpture of jagged edges and surfaces, in her rolled up white sweat pants. Adrián was building sandcastles, near his mother, using half-liter cans of San Miguel as battlements. I watched the scene, crouching on a rock, savoring the aroma of seaweed from the bay. The sea, the stillness of junk, the mangled car that had appeared so suddenly, not long ago, on the sand. There were still three blond swimmers in the water, their bleached hair radiant and fluorescent in the peaceful evening. They seemed to remain in the water because they couldn't convince a single wave to sweep them to shore. Crooknose and his buddies, paddling and bowing their heads.

So, here you are.

Crooknose. Now, I was sure. It was him. His arrogance and gesticulations gave him away even so far off at sea. He was at the other end of the beach, showing off with his discolored pals.

Adrián was waiting for his mother, who, with the sea swirling around and hiding her feet, was lifting a dripping postcard from the water. She let the drops fall onto the sand from one corner as she held it with scientific care. She dragged the postcard through the loose dry sand, which had still not been reached by the tide, and flipped it over like a croquette. From her pocket she pulled a plastic baggie and placed the postcard inside with the same care as a forensic police detective gathering hair from the scene of a crime. The men with the bleached blond heads had put on clean shorts under their dry swimming trunks. They'd already sheathed their boards. The Blonds were leaving the sand, hurriedly tripping and stumbling, not wanting to be caught by the dark. Crooknose's friends had already left and he was now walking along the beach talking into his cellphone, flipping his cigarette butt onto the sand, like a field marshal on vacation. I was still crouching on my rock, increasingly tense and ready to pounce. The detox patient with the postcard in the baggie shouted at her son to pick up the cans spread out over the sand, which would otherwise be swallowed up by the tide within a couple of hours. Now they were all gone, like the sun. All that remained were the Zen ruins of the tower, impassive and proudly holding its ground on the beach, the rusted heap of the car, Crooknose, and me.

FORTY-THREE
JELLYFISH

The French girl was the muse. Bands of hedonists flock to the Greek islands from all corners of the world, when they know it's summertime. They hope to bathe in the warm, crystal clear Mediterranean sea, polluted like any other, but only in certain places. They come to be seen. The eyes that normally follow them are no longer useful to them. They strut about like migratory birds, knowing they are exotic as they travel. But if their gazes cross and certain eyes rise to challenge them, they do so only to be sure they are being observed with envy and greed. The DJs enhance and endanger the lounge-chair siestas, the lunches and sundry cocktails from sunup to sundown, from moonup to moondown, and moonup to sunup, while Autumn seems like it will never arrive. Women in tangas, hairless men, mud sculptures waiting to be baked, dogs fresh from the parlor and cats rummaging through the trash, dining à la carte on the leftovers of exorbitant platters. *Sin musa, no hay medusas.* The French girl, her boyfriend, but most importantly, her breasts, camped out in front of the Stevensons, father and son, who were not camping in the strict sense of the word. Their rare reunions were always bizarre. It's true they'd paid for a campsite in the most beautiful campgrounds on That Island for a couple nights, that is to say, an undetermined number between three and five. Stevenson, in an act of compassion, had decided to take his father on a trip, convinced that he was starting to dodder. Their campsite was pitched to the extent that they'd laid out two towels on the grass. Poor Mr. Stevenson, for some time now, swore that he'd seen mermaids in the sea and scorpions on the beaches. The French girl with her boobs and boyfriend, on the other hand, were top-notch campers. Tent, table, tarp, and a gas stove. All the equipment necessary to avoid having

109

to leave the campsite for as long as they wanted to stay. Collapsible chairs, paddles, balls, and toiletries. Stevenson and his father were drinking in Cartesian style, from noon until close to fainting. Stevenson was sure that this family custom would facilitate harmony and buffer the news he was about to deliver to his father, that he was about to place him in a luxurious home on The Island, but that he planned to visit every week. They had been treated to the incredible spectacle of seeing their new neighbors, more precisely, the French girl, the muse, in all her splendor. Squatting and jumping, spreading tarps, pounding stakes, shaking towels, and scrubbing out a portable cooler after rinsing it out with the delicious freedom permitted by her miniscule, loose-fitting lace bikini. The French girl and her bust, in which the Stevensons, father and son, could have lived for months, not without certain inconveniences, came to form part of their vacation. It was no longer necessary for her to be present to be on their minds at breakfast or when proposing toasts. The muse and her curves were well aware of it, as was her boyfriend, no doubt. She, or they, carried this knowledge with belligerent and insolent indifference. Then one day, the three of them approached the family campsite to ask for a bottle of wine, a full one if possible. The Stevensons fell to pieces, between restrained gesticulations and sideways glances, as they rummaged through towels and sparse clothing, all filthy, until they found what had been requested. The muse wore a beach wrap, down below, and a damp, colorful bikini top that spoke loudly and, from behind which, her nipples peered out, smiling at the two clumsy searchers who nodded their heads without hearing that there wasn't a damned supermarket open that Sunday. After eating they sat disagreeably on the dock, in silence, distant, bored, Stevenson watched as his father took slugs from a bottle of wine in the hot sun without wearing a hat. "Be careful," he said over his shoulder as he went for a swim in the sea. He wasn't able to leave him, but he couldn't stand him either, nor could he take responsibility for him. He had a hard enough time caring for the cat. He let the shifting tide carry him elsewhere. Planting his feet, with his swim trunks in his hand, he summoned the French girl in his imagination and immediately she appeared in beach towel but no bikini top, smiling, purring, obeying Stevenson's every impulse as soon as he felt it. Her breasts, now uncovered, were like just-baked cupcakes: plump, warm, swollen and sweet. The undulations and perverse insinuations whispered into his ear by the French girl, inside his sun-stricken and red-wine-lulled mind, ultimately and overwhelmingly excited him. The sea wasted no time in attracting a jellyfish which, with its bloom, sank its long translucent filaments into him. Stevenson's father, without having to look into his son's eyes, knew what had happened. They knew each other too well, their trip had lasted too long. He felt pity, but also, in some way, pride. After finishing the wine and tossing his cigar butt, he dove into the water from the dock, leaving his clothes piled in a corner. Mr. Stevenson looked for a nice secluded spot where the waves were gentle. It had been a long time since he felt this way. His temples were throbbing, madly disordering his thoughts. He sought the muse, lightly closing his eyes, not too tightly, just enough to let the yellow light of the afternoon shine through his lids. When he found her, his mouth was dry and the muse was crouching at his feet, wrapping herself around his thighs and staring at him with the eyes of a cat. She clumsily covered her breasts, which acquired a forbidden dimension, partially concealed by the girl's fingers, as she asked him in French to bite her just a little. The good thing about a fantasy is that you can understand any language. Stevenson could not make himself understood in the campground as he tried to find a telephone to call an ambulance. The French girl and her boyfriend, their mouths open, tried to help but they couldn't calm him down. Stevenson's father's eyes were turned inward as he lay on the shore. Another jellyfish could be seen spreading out near the dock like clear squid ink.

FORTY-FOUR
RUBÉN

"Rubén?! How are you?!"

"Hey, what's up? Long time, man, no? How's it going?"

I had just tied Crooknose to the remains of a smashed car on the beach with his own leash, waiting for high tide, but it didn't seem like a good idea to mention it over the phone.

"Fine, everything's fine here on The Island. Where are you, man?"

"In The Valley, where am I going to be? It's started to snow, ooh, it's a promising year. You coming or what?"

"Well, yea, to tell the truth that would be good for me."

"What do you mean good for you? What's up?" Ruben, after a silence, toned down his Andalusian accent. "Well, come as soon as you can. You know you can sleep comfortably here on the sofa."

"Yea, okay. Hell yes! I'll tell you all about it… if you give me a place to crash for a few days, that would be great"

"To hell with it, get your ass over here."

Rubén doesn't judge, he only gives his opinion when asked, and then he skins me alive. When I tell him about it, he'll tell me the cretin with the broken nose had it coming to him. He'll fix his trial-pending eyes on me, and his smile will shadow the rest of his face. He'll throw away whatever he's smoking and then order another round. It's not a bad plan. To squat on Rubén's sofa, switch from salt to ice, from neoprene to feathers, from one board to another. From beach to mountain, water to water. The burning cars, the arrests, the mass evictions of the *Piolet*, they separated us the way they once united us. Although our idea of the world was pretty screwed up, it was also right on. When he needs me, I'll be there for him too. It's been a while since Rubén headed for the snow, hunting it down, and there he made a place for himself.

Rubén hasn't emerged from his canyon for six years. He doesn't want to know anything about the plains or the flatlands. After two seasons, I followed him, when I'd had enough of Epicentro, and we shared everything we could for the next four winters.

FORTY-FIVE
TO THE OTHER SIDE

You put a whole lot of kisses in a glass jar. It took a long time to put the kisses on pieces of paper. No two kisses are alike. It was a surprise. Your voice trembled over the phone when you sent one your indecipherable clues. To get my present I had to come by your house. Which would have been a pleasure, except we were separated by three thousand kilometers. I was running late and was only thinking of you as I flew down the highway an inch off the asphalt. I didn't blink an eye until I reached Epicentro airport. Airport security had specific instructions on how to battle tedium in the terminals. They didn't find anything of value in my bag. I always keep the good shit on me. I reached the Company sign-in office. I convinced a crew to take me to The Island. I boarded a plane and I think I slept for a while before we landed at Los Ambages airport. There I repeated the process, avoiding a search of my bag at security checkpoint "C." They were already searching someone else's bags.

The airport's name has to do with the maneuvers systematically executed by the planes as they approach the runway. At the end of the 1960s, during the tourist boom, a famous Belgian architect was hired to study The Island in order to design and locate an airport. The Belgian spent most of his time on the beaches and clubs at the time, seducing young male Mencey descendants, rather than working on the project. He died suddenly, an elderly man and, therefore, considered respectable. The media underplayed the fact that he was found tied to his bed with a plastic Alteza Supermarket shopping bag covering his head. The official cause of death left no room for doubt: cardiorespiratory failure. Among his belongings, tossed into a pile of overturned drawers, they found no jewels, watch, or gold pen, but they did find some papers outlining the project he was working on. The authorities discovered a map of The Island covered with incomprehensible notes and a large X indicating the spot where the airport now lies. They deduced that the document was the fruit of much orographic and meteorological study and the X marked the ideal spot for construction of the airport. They hired another architect to design a building, and he came up with a convincing design within a couple of weeks. They built it. Since the terminal's opening, all reports suggest that the X on the map of The Island marks the most dangerous spot for construction of an airport. Wind, obstinate fog, a circle of inconvenient mountains, and the rainiest area in the archipelago. Any unmarked area would have been better. I left the airport, called you, but you didn't answer your phone. So I went to your house. A long half hour. I was eager to breathe the humid, lush air. On the way I could smell the passion fruit, savoring the serenity that drew me to your house. I called you.

"Hello, sweetie, I'm on my way.

"Oh."

There, you didn't give me a kiss. Dry as an unwatered almond tree. Quite distant, quite different. I could see your house from the slope. I looked for the key you kept hidden under a rock in the garden and I entered. I didn't even have time to take off my backpack. On the dining room table, a clear glass jar with a metal lid, originally meant for holding tea, cookies, or pot buds, now filled with small white squares. Pieces of folded paper, almost all identical. Beside the jar, on the table, illuminated by two purple candles smelling of peat, lemon and peppermint, there was a note from you with what looked like the rules of the game. I flicked it away and it fell under the table. I opened the jar, redolent of you, and took out one of the pieces of paper. The only one tied with fine gauge twine for stringing together chunks of meat. *Welcome kisses.* I smiled. I know because I saw my own soft face, tongue hanging out, when I caught my reflection in the mirror. I took off my backpack, grabbed the jar, which was cold, and stared at it. My mouth watered as if I'd been given a kilo of anchovies, well-pickled in vinegar. You hadn't even gotten home but you'd already kissed me. I opened the jar again and put my hand in, which got stuck. It took me a while to get it out. I imagined living a normal life with my hand forever stuck inside a transparent jar submerged in your kisses, which I would never be able to read. For sure, if this were the case, I'd receive good disability benefits. I touched them the same way I ran my fingers through your recently showered infinity, slowly, stealing the dampness contained within. I began to open them as if you had never kissed me. As if no one had ever caressed my lips. As if I had only seen such scenes at the end of films. *Kisses at high tide. White kisses.* The possibilities were infinite. *Fantasy kisses with crushed ice.* It sounded like the specialty of the house at a fine restaurant. I grabbed others. *Kisses on your eyelids. Wasabi kisses. Why-don't-you-come-live-with-me kisses. Dolphin kisses. Upside-down on-top-of-you kisses. Mezcal worm kisses. Kisses without reason.* I was sure I wasn't doing it right. I picked the instructions up from the floor and saw there that I'd been committing an unlawful and delicious abuse. When you arrived I embraced you and returned all the kisses I'd read so far. I know there's one reserved for the end. It's written in the instructions. It's tied with fine twine, like the first—but don't get your hopes up—you thought out loud. Perhaps I'll open it last. I put them all carefully back so I could savor them later. They're always folded up, some have small marks, or quotation marks, or combinations of words that I've only read upon your fingers.

Forty-six
Puddles

I was walking through Epicenter again. A Sunday morning after a heartily enjoyed breakfast, I left the hotel to lose myself among the streets crammed with tourists and closed businesses. On the other hand, the shops selling novelty T-shirts printed in English ("Tourist triathlon: eating, drinking, fucking"... "Vodka: connecting people"), presided over by Pakistanis enthusiastically and unflinchingly hawking bootleg jerseys of the city's top soccer team, seemed to never close. I stumbled into a serious exhibit of works by Dalí and I snuck in by jumping the turnstile at the entrance, saving myself the coins they demanded. A curious selection: the Valencian *falla* Dalí designed, a collection of sculptures he created by commission, photographs of a downed helicopter, Dalí with a stuffed horse he had brought up to his room at a Hilton Hotel, after rejecting a flesh-and-blood steed they brought to room 508, the Anthropomorphic Cabinet, and a whole lot of crockery. Along general lines, surrealism should be disagreeable, it is composed of the same disquieting texture as dreams you would never describe to anyone else, and we thank you for that. Dreams always have some meaning, but we very rarely know what that is. Dalí never painted the sea very well, although he knew how to dilute time with water. Surrealism has always been gobbled up by global markets to the point of deserving its own section in large department stores. Whoever has never really stared at a painting (which, in itself, might be quite beneficial), except for scenes of hunting on the British landscape with which they adorn their bungalows along the Suntan Coast, speaks of surrealism when they find themselves witnessing a scene that is simply strange, and not necessarily shocking. They also use it when referring to something they don't understand, or perhaps only partially, stripping it of its subversive threat.

I stopped to have a coffee. A pimp, who epitomized himself perfectly, played with the stub of a cigar, surrounded by six or seven of his girls. They were attempting the impossible: not to be noticed. There were uniformed and plainclothes police patrolling the busy streets, bustling with extravagant, extra-verboten, extroverted beings. The girls are what they are, and even if they act demure, they will always look the same. They smoke like whores and watch the boss in the same way as he refuses to toss away his cigar but keeps lighting it over and over. His belly obliges him to sit a certain distance from the table and none of the girls are willing to look him in the eye. Money is the worst thing that ever happened to us. The old men of the neighborhood go off with one or another of the whores. With the slender blond with black teeth, or the plump Moroccan. Today they're looking for them at their spots on the corners of three or four streets, but they aren't there. After searching for them, they're surprised to find them sitting around this table, in the company of the pimp with his satisfied smile as he carries out, *in situ*, his market study. He sends one of the girls to pay for the drinks with only ten euros. The old guys can't help but stare at the girls' thighs, and then at the fat guy, and when their necks have craned to their maximum torsion, their stares go plop in the puddles behind them, on the uneven sidewalks, the armored vehicles of the cleaning services. I continue walking and step on some fresh dog turd. I suppose and hope it is a turd from a large dog. I wash my flip-flops in a puddle, a large puddle, but the stink accompanies me the rest of the afternoon. The street narrows at a cross street where there's an old church. A circus trailer with a Slovak name, towed by a van, is blocked by another car, trapped in a bottleneck formed between the buildings and the filthy sidewalks. The car is from the East, the 1970s, all right angles, spotted with rust, tinted glass, and a sub-Saharan driver who sits quietly perspiring. His silence is owed to his lack of a driver's license, visa, ID card or work permit. He stares at the button that activates the horn on the steering wheel and shrugs his shoulders as the police, who have appeared on the scene by rappelling down the walls of the buildings all around, attempt to clear the way. All of this is well-seasoned by six or seven simultaneous first communions for neighborhood girls who emerge exhilarated from the penetration of Christ in their bodies and through the gothic door, exhausted in large part from the heat. Accompanying the recently communed—dressed in the prototypes of what will years later be their wedding dresses—are their families. The girls, the mothers, the aunts, the cousins, in cream colors, and the men, the fathers, godfathers and stepfathers, all relentlessly take photographs with different devices, cursing as they glance sideways at the negligence of drivers and urban security. I decide to flee the scene knowing it will never be resolved. I'm disappointed that no little girl is trying out, or falling off, her new bicycle, to crown the chaos, or that the trainers have not lost one of their ligers (a type of animal that only lives on circus billboards, a cross between a furry lioness and an incandescent Bengal tiger).

Forty-seven
I Don't Like Your Umbrella

One afternoon, when it was raining as if for the last time, you were walking with me in sandals, with an umbrella, not saying a word. In the van, parked on a side street, now well into Saturday night, you dried your feet with a towel I'd found in the trunk. They'd just spent the day avoiding puddles and being stomped on. I thought I knew how far I could get. I dropped into a squat and grabbed a foot at random, the left. I took it and let the towel drop to the floor and put it in my mouth without saying a word. You started looking around nervously through the open door, pushing me away with your hand, but I insisted. A couple of kids chasing each other ran past but didn't notice us. A married couple sharing an umbrella, huddling together, hurried past us. I didn't stop until you pushed me hard, "Stop it, dumbass. They're filthy from the puddles!"

I nodded, my mouth filled with toes. Perhaps I shouldn't have smiled as you put on your shoes, reprimanding me in a screechier tone than usual. Then, much later in a bar, we argued because we had nothing more important to talk about. I never liked people with umbrellas. They let anyone carry one, like being a parent, although it's not your fault. It's a lack of respect for all of us who defend ourselves from the rain with hoods. You umbrellists, you spread the ribs of your artifacts like turkey tails, displaying your bold colors, scorning the stormy grays, brandishing them like fencing students. You spoke to me, without looking me in the eye, referring to maypops, *passiflora caeruleas*, and how in the rest of the world they're known as passion fruit. I was trying to tell you that I wanted you all to myself, but you were already distant and ordering the check.

Forty-eight
Rain

Rain, gently falling through a night spent driving on the highway. An old highway, tattooed with tragic skid marks, venomous tangents on the curves. At dawn, while everyone still sleeps, I roll along, calm and collected. On the radio, El Niño de La Selva sings that no one is lord of their final morning. I'm going to stop at the next gas station. I'll have a second breakfast, my trip is a little more than half over, so I'll be in the valley of snow before noon. Rubén is waiting for me and on The Island they're asking questions I don't want to answer. A blanket of snow fell two days ago and the cold is so blue it should help keep the snow creamy. Sometimes, when sliced through by blades, the snow sounds like the powder at the start of a vinyl record: the exact moment when the needle tries to find the groove, but still jumps the concentric track. It's been eight o'clock for the last hour. It's raining much harder now. In the passenger seat, strapped in by the seatbelt: my glass jar, or your glass jar, with your kisses, or my kisses. The brass lid protects the mauve-colored piece of paper you prepared. On the mountain, it might be snowing hard. Large flakes are already falling from the sky. That mountain is responsible for more than one of my gray hairs. I take curve number 712, humming along with the melody on the radio. I enter curve 713, calm, absorbed in the song, when the back of the van starts to float. First it wiggles lasciviously and then it cuts a diagonal, sliding into the curve. I spin the steering wheel. Should I brake? I turn into the skid and now I'm sliding the other way. The wheels do nothing but skim over the water and ice. I step on the accelerator to see if that will help. The van is completely sideways as we enter curve 713, out of control. In a heretofore unknown time structure, the nanoseconds elongate and the music cryogenicizes in a shrill cry with sampler. What

I see through the windshield I've already seen a hundred times in afternoon movies. Now I'm upside down and the noise of the van's top scraping the asphalt drowns out everything else. Sparks fly like fireworks. The Moment vibrates, charmed like a snake. I tell myself, this is it. My whole life does not pass before my eyes, but I do get excited. I smile slightly as I cling to the steering wheel. I hold my body tight, now a homogenous unit without arms, bones, eyes, or innards. I explode. Shattered in a thousand dispersed pieces only to immediately reunite, pieces spitting themselves out, then returning me to the van, now deformed.

I bounce off the median. One, two, three metal bars bent over like licorice sticks. I come to a stop about fifty meters from the first impact, sensing that I'm okay. The van flips again and lands upright with the wheels on the asphalt. Sitting sideways in the center lane I pat myself up and down, maybe I'm not so well. I check all the vital spots I can think of. I get out of the car to check the damage, I get back into the van, I try to start it despite the fact that an enormous puddle is forming below the engine and the smoke rising from it smells like a funeral wreath laid at a sharp curve. Your jar topples out the open door and rolls away. I chase after the glass, steadfastly rolling downhill, crossing all three lanes of the highway. I capture it unbroken, hermetically sealed, with all your kisses shaken up like a pot of popcorn over the flame, like a bingo barrel at the start of a game.

I kick the battered driver's side door six times, cursing my luck. That'll fix it. Not a single car has passed by yet. I kick the tires. I wish I knew how to cry. The situation calls for it and maybe I do too. I turn off the music, the radio is undamaged. The water has screwed me royally. Later the highway patrolman will call it hydroplaning, without even getting out of his car so that his uniform won't get wet as he fills out the report and asks me for my documents. Acting like a good cop, he'll offer me a cigarette. I haven't smoked in a week. I accept without thinking about it. Now it's all so easy. But what if I had stopped at the previous gas station? What if I'd slept more? What if this had happened fifty kilometers from here, in the canyon? What if I've ruptured my spleen without realizing it? What if this is the day I die? Did I step on the brakes? What if I hadn't stepped on the brakes? What if the van didn't have rear-wheel treason? And what if I'd stepped on the brakes? What if there weren't any median? What if I'd had a passenger? What if I'd been going faster? What if there hadn't been any ice on the asphalt? What if I start to cry? What if I hadn't taken a cigarette from the cop? What if I'd closed my eyes and screamed in the middle of all that duck-tailing? What if a car had been coming from behind? What if I wake up connected to a bunch of tubes? What if I never reach Rubén's sofa? What if, what if... Easy Rider.

FORTY-NINE
BON VOYAGE

A good trip is one during which you attempt to verify something, like searching for a color you dreamt of, or an aroma you only know by its description, or an image that fulfills a desire. The poet does not put wild animals to sleep as if he were a tamer, but continues along his way, the traveler who does not think of himself but rather of the voyage, of sleepy shores, of forests of hands, of animals imbued with souls. What is difficult is not attaining what you desire, but rather to desire. From the victorious position of being desirous, if you don't have something, you conquer it.
Gilles Deleuze

I found this on a wall. On the highway, waiting for a mechanic's diagnosis, as the van stood by, suffering and crumpled. I found it written in black spray paint, a quick but meticulous work of art. Someone was trying to communicate with me. I asked after it in some bookshops, but they had hardly heard of him.

FIFTY
THE SISTERS

Is it good to save your life? All you manage to do is postpone the inevitable, although, of course, it's especially fortunate if you can avoid the Plegia sisters: Hemi, Para and Quadri.

FIFTY-ONE
LIQUIDITY

Poverty around here is measured by how much money you have to spend on a given day. It's hard not to spend fifty in twenty four hours. They charge you that just to be here, just to exist. It's also measured in how many patrons you can find from one dawn to the next. You can steal toilet paper from the ski area bathrooms and you can manage to crap as often as possible at friends' houses or bars just after they open, which is when the bathrooms are still clean. You can steal sugar packets by the fistful from cafés. I don't think they'd ever call the cops on you for that since it's more of a nuisance than anything else, but it's a good idea to distract whoever's working the morning shift in as you order a complicated coffee, obliging them to turn around several times as they prepare it behind the bar. To that end I recommend ordering a *desgraciado* (decaf, skim milk, saccharin). And then there's the firewood. At Rubén's house we use the fireplace for the holy days of obligation, or when somebody comes over and their eyes open wide: "Son of a bitch, you can see your breath in this house!" Or after I've gone out on a raid. Firewood raids are complicated. They have to be precise, subtle, you have to hoodwink the old man and the entire village, which silently watches everything, passing in front of the woodshed as if it were everyone's civic duty. The old man puts the wood on an enormous scale big enough to weigh a thousand kilos. He uses a hanging scale, well-rusted over a hundred winters. No doubt, everything is weighed with a thumb on the scale. When you tell him to stop, he decides on the weight and the price. The value of the wood is never the same. A hundred ten kilos, twenty euros; a hundred six, twenty-five. The old man always wears the same frayed rope as a belt and a green V-neck sweater, worn through at the elbows. He, whose mattress is stuffed with paper money of every color and decade, would never go to the pharmacy to buy something for his fever blisters. He would never get a filling for one of those molars dangling from his gums when he yawns. But this same old man will give you a hand whenever you have to carry off some firewood. He suffers from lumbago but feels slightly guilty about gouging customers for a few chunks of wood that aren't even dry. It's at that moment, as the old man is throwing logs into my trunk, that I grab all I can from the enormous pile of firewood he keeps under a tarp. The stuff he hasn't weighed out, which isn't green, which he only sells to preferred customers. He loads a couple of logs, giving me a hand, and I try to snag some extra logs to battle the extreme chill in Rubén's house. The temperature outside at three in the afternoon is thirty-six degrees; the temperature inside: thirty. Another way I can shift the economic scales in my favor is to shoplift in the local supermarkets. They raise their prices by thirty percent alleging that to bring their products here they have to be transported by truck, crossing a narrow canyon where the sun never shines and where the asphalt is covered with ice. They openly make this claim, a claim, like any other, but in order for me to be here I had to travel on that same road. I go to the supermarket bundled up in baggy clothes with lots of pockets because it's winter and very cold. The loot you bring home depends mostly on your skill, the impression you leave on the cashiers, and your clean record. Rubén, for example, is no longer permitted even to enter any food establishment in the valley. He used to be fast and skillful, but he was also susceptible to greed and was caught by surprise one Christmas Eve as he was trying to make off with a cured ham under his down jacket. A horrible black toe nail was sticking out from just below his ear as if it were an earring. To avoid dying of starvation I've spent the last few weeks trying to find someone who'd like to benefit from my limited productive abilities. I've cleaned stairwells, smiled for interminable lengths of time in hotel lobbies, I've even worn a clown nose so the spoiled children of wealthy families who come to this snowland, dressing their offspring in tommy hillfiger, periodically giving them perms to perpetuate their Bourbon look, could be entertained in the afternoons while their parents were resting or drinking hot wine or spending money in the village. Necessity seems to lead me down side roads. I once worked in Graus. I only worked there for one night, during carnival celebrations, when temperatures are generally below freezing. Young people wear their ski jackets and windbreakers over their costumes of Indians, gangsters, and lewd bishops. They drink themselves silly as the band plays, roughly speaking, timeless classics for all the neighbors to hear. *Un Tractor Amarillo* and *Mierda De Ciudad*, to placate the tastes of kids on amphetamines wearing only T-shirts. *Como Una Ola*, *Sabor De Amor*, and *Paquito El Chocolatero*. All sung by choirs swaying leisurely from side to side for long performance hours, changing colors thanks to the lights and the whiskey, hiding behind plumes of smoke aimed by the stagehands. Then the house DJ takes over with recorded music for these events. I got home at two in the morning. Earlier, I'd been working at the hotel, and before that at the chairlifts. At eight o'clock on the dot I came out from behind the right side of the bar, where I served mega-overpriced mixed drinks. Since it was obvious they didn't pay me what I was worth and as I believe in fair trade, I occasionally pocketed a fifty rather than putting it in the cash register. Between one thing and another I got paid triple and then some, so I left quite happily. Before leaving, I saw how one chick was being treated at the door: "That one is the worst from Venta de Puértolas." And she spat back, trying not to clench her jaw, "Hey! I'm not from there, I'm from way past there."

Then she spotted a ten-euro bill all covered in dirt and she picked it up and kissed it, obscenely running her kalimotxo-coated tongue all over it, enveloping it in her steamy breath, and announced, "I'll spend this tomorrow." She kissed the bill some more. "This baby I'll spend on ice cubes."

FIFTY-TWO
SIX TEARS

You cried. Six salty tears. Three from each eye. You cried in the traditional way, but I wasn't there. You don't cry in your worst moments, or when rage washes over you. Deaths and misfortunes leave you dry. Once, when you were little, you thought you would never again be seen with damp eyes, and this blocked your tear ducts. But excess liquid in the sockets has to be drained once in a while. So, one day you're watching a soap opera and you begin to cry inconsolably when they give the weather report, and not because of the lack of snow or the rising sea. Or one afternoon, wandering aimlessly, you have to find a secluded spot along the street, where no one will surprise you, sobbing, trying to recompose yourself. This time it was a TV-movie. A film both bad and poignant, a film as anodyne as only television can make them. The kind that's calculated to fill your eyes with tears. It had been two years since the previous time. You cried quietly, without wild gestures, sensing how six intrepid salty tears spilled screaming down your cheeks. You began to breathe easier.

FIFTY-THREE
MOTHERLODE

In an attempt to be a productive unit, this morning I shoveled the snow that had accumulated on what is left of my van. A meter of giant snowflakes, delicately settling one on top of another through the night. The ground, a still white layer, a treacherous mirror of indestructible ice. When I managed to clear the way, I started to leave for the ski rental shop where I've been working in the mornings in return for some pocket change. Rubén appeared at the side of my van, his boots unbuckled, his eyes bloodshot, tongue hanging out.

"Did you see how much came down?"

"Yes, Rubén, I've got retinas too, but I have to go to work."

His tongue still protruding, his mouth formed a diabolic smile that seemed to spit, "Stop complaining!" I quickly became angry because this cosmic fortuity had bestowed upon him—on his morning off—this motherlode of fluffy, promiscuous snow, but in spite of everything I grabbed my board and drove the van back into the snow and off we went to the slopes. There we use the lifts only to get from one stand of trees to another where we deflower the sought after slopes. The tourists, out of laziness, fear, and cold, have hardly gone up the mountain, and the locals, well, they have to work. Our tongues hardened and turned purple at the end of each run. Drop-offs, woods, jumps into the void and landings in three meters of virgin snow. No way you can keep your tongue in its place. At close to two in the afternoon, with no more sustenance than some broth, two coffees, and some of Rubén's weed, I went down and grabbed the shovel again, dug out the van, again, and went to the rental shop, my clothing still dripping ice. It was convincing enough that they didn't fire me. The manager had also had problems getting his car on the road. But he'd been there since ten-thirty in the morning. I reminded them that, since the accident, my van didn't always start, or it dripped oil, or it left me stranded every few days. But it wasn't convincing enough for them to send me home for some dry clothes. I was fixing bindings, changing lightbulbs, waxing boards, and taking out trash until dinnertime. The manager has all kinds of tics, too many for someone who is just beginning his mid-life crisis. He'll end up shooting some of his clients during the off-season with his father's shotgun, but he still changes his watch often. He likes to show-off his watch collection to his employees. So, he has something to spend his profits on. I'm like a goat, going from one side of the house to the other. I was going to go to bed, limping, but instead, I opened the drawer and took out the jar. I removed the purple packing paper you put there to keep the other pieces of paper from getting ruined with the passage of time and I grabbed a handful. The series began with some *Cosmic kisses* (like the good fortune that was granted to Rubén). On the second piece of paper I received *Nihilist kisses*, and then *Earthquake kisses*. While my smile was selling its soul to the devil, it began to shine thanks to the ice. *Kisses for eating my feet. Childish kisses. Kisses on the washing machine.* I turned back to the first pages of my Log, seeing you lying in the sun, myself at your feet, between your legs. Immediately, you offered me handwritten *Kisses for your pecker.* I could feel them. I spread my legs a little so you could give me kisses more comfortably and a big smile spread across my face. *Obese and obsessive kisses.* You ended with *Sprinkled kisses.* I prepared some toast with butter and jam, topped with pieces of paper recently removed from the jar.

FIFTY-FOUR
ANY OLD HOUSE

We arrived at a house, any old one. We dropped our baggage and hugged each other urgently. After all those absurd moments, run through with desire, clinging to nothingness. Come. I'm coming. Come now. I'm coming. When are you coming? When I can. Any old house, absolute silence, a ray of light passing through the blinds, standing face to face. Staring into one another without blinking, passing our hands over each other's face and hair. We undress each other slowly. Dizzy. Unbuttoning buttons, loosening belts, raising arms, removing clothing. Undressing one another like peeling the skin from an orange all in one piece, reaching nudity interrupted, as pants drop to shoes on the floor. Kicking feet into the air, shoes bouncing off the walls in the hallway. Clothes flying out the door. Again, we embrace, ferociously. Again, that heat, radiating from your belly like iron born in a forge. But, first, let's wrinkle the covers on the sofa, brew some coffee, snoop through the drawers, sow the living room with strands of tobacco, move the pictures around on the walls, sample the bar. Tell me about your life, it's been a long time.

FIFTY-FIVE
BATH HOLE

The wasps hover conspicuously over the little snow left on the most miserly outcroppings. Rubén and I decide to go to the spa, which won't open for another couple of months, to soak in the hot sulfur spring they have outside. Legal authorities dictate that any exploiter of thermal springs must leave a stream running beyond a given perimeter for free and accessible use by mortals who do not wish to pay for this service of nature. We park the van at a distance where a thirty-meter snowdrift spills onto the road and blocks us from driving further. Then, up the half-undressed mountain, we follow the path taken by an avalanche and we admire how a cross road has blocked its otherwise implacable progress toward the thalasso-rural-relax hotel. An affectionate couple is already in the hot spring. She tries to sink down into the water, but it's too late, we've already seen her large, dark pink nipples, hard and erect, in delicate contrast to her pale skin. Not just a topless woman but a woman bathing with a backdrop of all of winter and water covering her up to her belly. Ruben and I stop howling and chasing our tails (each chasing his own) long enough to ask the couple how much longer they're staying. The sun is getting low, but there's still some afternoon left. The ridgeline will soon block the sun's rays. We take a walk to let the couple kiss, smoke and get out of there. Rubén passes the time smoking as if waiting in ambush. The couple is gone. The water in the spring is calm, except for the stealthy trickle of water keeping it full, spilling from a corroded black hose that winds toward the main building of the spa from where the smell of a musty fireplace emanates. Drawing lots, I get to bathe first. Meanwhile, Rubén smiles at the sun as it bids us farewell, sinking between two slopes. Rubén knows he will die buried in the mountain and that provides him with the serenity so many of us desperately seek in our struggle against the fear of plunging downward. We agree on a half hour each as night is fast approaching. A half hour is normally about forty-five to fifty minutes. The water holds steady at seventy-three degrees despite the fact that it's a late winter afternoon in the mountains. I undress and slide into the hole with a rock from the mountain so I'll have a clean place to plant my butt. It's a built-in tub, although deeper than most. Only one person fits, and there are absolutely no frills. Two people can only fit one on top of the other, facing the same direction, or seated face to face, crotch to crotch. Neither Rubén nor I is willing to make the effort to share it. To submerge yourself in that water is to disappear bit by bit. The heat of the water and the acoustic isolation provide very agreeable levels of intimacy. Raising your head back to the surface brings shock to your face from the brutal cold of the air. Everything smells a bit of rotten eggs thanks to the sulfur. You hardly notice, but the body relaxes like when you unfasten a belt. We talk about women, different things about them, but mostly their butts, their breasts. We love them dearly, although Rubén complains they're all liars. You can just look at a woman's boobs to know if she's telling the truth. They're never what they appear to be. If their boobs are sagging, they tighten their waists, if they're small, they stuff them, and if they're gigantic, well, if they're gigantic, they lord them over you. We still haven't gotten into the question of surgery because we hold fast to the natural female breast with its fascinating abilities of movement. Putting plastic beneath the skin can't be a good thing. The swaying of a woman in a bikini on the beach opens the gateway to the imagination which is the floodgate of a dam. In the end, Rubén doesn't trust them. I tell him about how when I first met you, you were nude, how you tasted of anvil, how you asked me to take tango lessons and I went willingly, about the jar of your kisses. Rubén smiles out loud.

"Buddy-y-y, you should see your face, the way you're talking."

Slowly, my voice is now a mere whisper on the surface of the water until Rubén whistles a couple of times, demanding his turn to bathe. I get out after an hour and fifteen minutes. We switch roles. He undresses.

"Now tell me, why did you come here so all of a sudden?"

"Oh, Crooknose." I go on to tell him about the bleached blond, his beach nationalism, our collisions, the crashed car on the beach, the swells and storm surges.

"Shit." Rubén clicks his tongue, glances at me, nods his head and disappears underwater. He surfaces with bubbles coming from his nose and a giant smile spreading across his face.

"As if the world needed another Crooknose."

I'm still drying off when a German shepherd suddenly appears in front of me, tapered snout, ears alert, his intentions uncertain. He watches us as Rubén moons him, changing position in the hole. When he sees the dog, he threatens him in *Bantúes*, his cock shrunken from the cold. The dog nods his head and disappears, running off in the direction from whence he came. Rubén settles back in the thermal water and, just as I'm about to put on my underwear, a couple of highlanders come into view, walking slowly in the face of this horror that has suddenly appeared before their eyes. My ass and a pair of boxer shorts at half-mast welcome them amid the foliage of this oasis. Silence falls, colder than the breeze that suddenly blows through. They continue on their way, glancing at us sideways, smiling, also sideways, but on the other side of their faces. An hour later, Rubén gets out, very mellow, mellow with water. The highlander couple reappears with their dog, heading in the opposite direction. Now that we're dressed and somewhat purple from the temperature, they don't hesitate to say hello and joke about us taking a mountain bath in early March. They mention that one shouldn't stay in a hot bath for more than twenty minutes and that any longer is dangerous for just about everything, especially stress. Our goal is now to correct the mistake by accompanying them to the hotel bar, where we order several rounds of coffee with cognac. Meanwhile, the dog prances about outside, chasing ghosts in the snow.

FIFTY-SIX
IT'S ALWAYS THE SAME

It's always the same. We'll go ten, fifteen, or twenty days without so much as smelling each other. Hearing each other only through the distortions of the telephone and the interference of desire. We think we're building something but the truth is that we are not passing much time together. Then we see each other and a hundred hours feels like too few. Studying each other's face we discover a new wrinkle, another furrow. During these visits it is urgency that reigns supreme. We protect ourselves against it by embracing the other. I finish packing my backpack as you watch, perched on the couch with your legs folded neatly beneath your trunk. Before going out the door, until who knows when, you wrap your soft-skinned cilantro arms around my neck and, like a spoilt child implore me, "Don't go." My answer is always the same, "You come." We get so sad and then we grow more wrinkles. I'm on the road with the sun leading me down the highway when I begin to remember. I remember you a step away from tears, in your pajamas, voluntarily helpless, saying, "Don't go." I remember also my shameless smile, brushing your cheek, and my answer, "You come." Over and over again. Then, when I stop for gas, I wonder how long it will be before we say it all in reverse:

"Don't come"

"Go."

Fifty-seven
Shipwreck

A choke collar with prongs turned inward, around the neck of a hunting dog. Sometimes embraces can be like that: virulent and blood-seeking. Lifesavers missing on the beaches, redemptive and orange, dust-covered in the trunk of some car, in some garage, or dusted off and decorating the walls of some seafood restaurant of an inland city. You cling to it, to be saved, to find refuge. Stupid embraces, like a tightly knotted tie at your throat. Then, there are those that are like attacks arising from the sewers of damaged hearts. Resentful, irritated and humiliated. A carnal embrace, like the aureole embracing the nipple of a young girl, the breast embracing the aureole, the hand delicately rocking the breast; a body embracing a breast, another body embracing the first body. Concentric and exponential embraces like Russian dolls. Sources of nutrition, generators, human shields, empirical verifications, crowns of affection. The essence arises from pressing a body as if it were the bulb of an antique perfume bottle. They close deals, keep flames alive, fireproofing some, leading to truces, taming shrews and gratifying with all their heart gestures, favors and details. On arctic landscapes they blend with first-aid techniques and are taught in clinics. Hair stands on end, anger is moderated, disputes defused, trails blazed, tears dried and spilled, nothing is done, and attempts are made to return to the womb from where we still don't know why we were evicted. We travel in space, time is crystalized, there's a gradual easing of the Ying, the Yang, and the muscles of masks worn by men and women, frozen with the fear of having their feet on the earth of a globe in flames. Necks and heads search and find, unfailingly, the hollow left exposed by the other's neck and head. We learn to give hugs when we are very small although soon thereafter we learn of their use as an organic weapon. We attach a label to them as prohibited substances and another warning of their dangerous contents.

Yesterday I embraced an administrative aid who suddenly seemed like a teddy bear: inert, squishy and chubby. I expected the odor of a man who was capable of anything, but when I squeezed a little bit, I only encountered the aroma of the softener used in his mother's home. At first, he turned red, which was not anger, but it wasn't red from embarrassment either. Then, when I didn't let him go, he tried to break loose without much effort, gently twisting. After a few moments of passive resistance, it was he who wouldn't let me go, squeezing me with his droopy arms. When he fell asleep, I set him down with the utmost care on the train tracks and left, without making a sound. From the window out back the purposeful crying of a baby emerges. He wants his ration, like everyone else in this world. Like all the world he wanders his own timeless world, no one lifts him from the crib, or cradles him in their arms. His rattles are now worthless and the toy monsters frighten him. What he needs is for someone close to him to give him the gift of holding him. He does not grow quiet and so I knock on the door, I offer to hold him in my own arms. I've just gotten out of the shower. Rarely have I been so soft, fragrant and hydrated. They throw me out of the house, beating me with spoons and threatening to call the police. Let them call, let them call, but the baby would prefer my embrace to that of a police officer, armed and with sweat rings on his shirt. Donate, take, lend, give, offer, request, concede, complain, reject, demand, beg, surrender, misplace, rent, lose, solicit, postpone, authorize, prescribe, reject embraces.

You begin with a finite number of embraces but you can't know if you'll give them all away, nor how many you'll receive.

FIFTY-EIGHT
ANTIOXIDANT

The world, then, corroded and rusty, so littered with rubble that it was only possible to discern some peace from a distance. Those who still believed in something, went from one ruined area to another by plane, and thus we had the opportunity to observe a sea of clouds above the amber sea. At an altitude of thirty thousand feet the destruction could pass unnoticed.

In the open jar there is still a good handful of kisses I've decided to cash in. I don't know when, nor at what price. With nothing better to do, I open it again and again. *Antioxidant kisses. Purple kisses. Terrorist kisses. Kisses in the spot that drives me crazy. Kisses on the tip. Loving kisses. Contaminating kisses. Thyme kisses. Kisses gone crazy. Kisses a little lower please. Kisses from the clouds. Surprise me kisses. Burning kisses. Vaginal kisses. Spicy kisses. Forming a square paper puzzle kisses. Bubbly kisses.* There are many more. *X-ray kisses. Searing kisses. Thousands of kisses. Suck my neck and take off my clothes kisses. Cardamom kisses. Brazilian kisses. Tender kisses. Tango rhythm kisses. Nude kisses.* I would have spent the rest of my life in that crystal jar, cushioned by pieces of paper with astonishing combinations of letters. *Naughty kisses. Sweet kisses. Kisses just because. From the garden kisses. Outrageous kisses. Against the wall kisses. By the fireplace kisses. Pudding kisses. On your back kisses. Kisses with tongue from sacral dimple to neck.* A crystal cage, too comfortable for a buzzard my size. *Impatient kisses. Torrential kisses. Tumbled kisses. I miss you kisses. Troubled kisses. Moist kisses. Timeless kisses.* I can feel your lips warm upon my face, just having them close. *Mellow kisses.* The metallic taste of your tongue as you slowly close your eyes. Your hands grasping the hair at the nape of my neck and calmly ordering me to give up. *Rough cat's tongue kisses.* Through your smooth clothing I feel your self-circling nipples observing me. *Caressing kisses. Candied kisses. Kisses that melt me. Drop-everything-come-let-me-eat-you kisses. Salty kisses. Kisses in the right armpit. Nibble-on-the-nipples kisses. Prisoner kisses. Intimate kisses. On the edge of the bathtub kisses. Discover me kisses! Cozy kisses. Dying of laughter kisses. Toasted kisses. Adrenaline kisses. Wait for me in the back kisses. Centrifugal kisses. Black kisses. Hungry upon your mouth kisses. Blindfolded kisses.* The muscles in your face relax, out of control. *Kisses like earthquakes. Quicksilver kisses. Watery kisses on your cock. Snack kisses.* Now, how can I face going outside?

FIFTY-NINE
SNOW

The wondrous fiction of mountain life is coming to an end for me. It's expensive. Technical apparel is always expensive. The valley is pretty much the same. The slopes have not lost a single degree. They've built more bungalows and keep stitching on more towers. I carve lines and curves through the snow with my 1'58 chisel. I've left my most ethereal track, expecting it to disappear with the thaw, or be delicately covered over by the next storm. I leave in the morning, well-fed, early, though not at the break of dawn, and I travel at the speed dictated by my board. When my body gets warm, I usually take a break. Enough for a coffee and to meet up with someone or something to accompany me on a few more runs. One morning I'm transformed, just like the snow crunching beneath my feet. I become a dragonfly and skim just a few millimeters above the white blanket, leisurely but blindingly fast. I sniff some stamens, ignore the pistils, and continue on my way, which changes at every curve. The other night they got me out of bed when I had just finally warmed my pajamas with the heat of my inner organs. We had a plan, which stalled. Then I realized that if it had stalled, it was only because it needed a running start. It was still before midnight and the moon was growing cold and covered with swell-headed inscriptions. Edurne appeared, smiling, and practically sat down on the jar.

"What is this?" she asked, looking me in the eye as I stared into the mist obscuring the road. Rubén snorted, his tone mocking.

"Nothing," I said. "Preserved kisses."

Rubén locked eyes with me. Edurne stared at the jar. They lifted it from the seat, carefully handling it and wrapping it in a cloth, and while one of them prepared something to smoke the other set to finding music on the radio. We started up Lala-ja mountain. They were grooming the snow nonstop. At dawn the resort must look like a giant postcard you could skate over. Enormous combines guarding a penitentiary. The darkness splashed in all directions, frozen, emanating from some vague center, the entire slope aglow. Silver-plated. We slipped past the machines, emboldened by the communal hum of some song. The moon was now glowing brighter in a sky empty of everything except blinking stars. On the way, Rubén slipped on a broad sheet of ice in the parking lot. When we returned, our mission accomplished, he slipped again in the same spot, but in the opposite direction. His backpack, with the board dangling from it, his helmet still on his head, his bulky clothing, all beneath the full moon, still immense, with the headlights of the caterpillars searching for us without knowing we were even there, made us fall to pieces laughing. Sharp laughter. The cold entering our throats and exiting as vapor into the night. We went up to where we were sure not to run into any machines. Lalaja was silent, the fresh-made corduroy snow meticulously groomed. Long grooves cut and compact, conserved as best as possible through the night so the week off would be a profitable reality in the morning. We had to trudge for a couple of hours since we hadn't left room in our backpacks for haste. Silence and cold night sweat. Edurne is a titan with the body of a fairy. It's the first time she's been on the board since she messed up her knee and had to stay inside for fifteen days. Now she goes crushing the crust of the fresh-scented snow. Rubén has a clear head and, determined, marches on. My eyes, without goggles, have adapted to the faint night light, exaggerated by the snow. All is blue: the sky, the mountain, the cold. All except the moon. Edurne doesn't believe in competition with anyone other than herself, so she's always striving for the tiebreaker. When we get tired, we take a break, catch our breath, and then, with our boards on our feet, we descend to the concealed van.

The ground gives way under our feet at an agreeable rhythm. We don't speak, it's enough to sense each other's presence. We stop. We sit on some comfortable rocks near the woods. We drink tea from a thermos, smoke and eat a piece of carrot cake Rubén has brought. It doesn't feel like Friday, but we're aware it's after two in the morning. The cold becomes painful now that we've stopped, and realizing this, we decide to keep going downhill. Rubén goes head first and we follow as if it was the last day of all days. We fly over ledges almost in a rage. Floating is merely an attempt to return to the placenta. Edurne takes the lead, she wants to deflower the snow that lies ahead. Everything happens slowly and gently. The cold in our faces and the darkness reflected on the snow combine for this sensation. Sweeping turns, empty of consciousness, destroying mountain walls just formed by the machines. The snow walls collapse like dominos, slower than expected, much slower than our desire. We agreed to remove our boards once we got to the bottom, with infinite discretion, and not to stop until we were in the van, safe from judges, guards and dogs. I glance sideways at Rubén and Edurne as we converge on the rendezvous, each from his or her own direction and at the pace of our respective breathing. They carry their boards under one arm, smiling broadly, staring at a constant present in the form of a highway lined with evergreens. Rubén again walks over the sheet of ice and again slips in slow motion, falling in the same place as when we set out, except in the opposite direction. Our stealthy style is lost. We laugh and end up rolling in the snow, squealing gleefully. Exhilarated, we climb into the van.

We get home, now quiet and sunk into that small depression you find yourself in when you've emptied your body of serotonin. Then we share a bed, Edurne creates a tie between us, then falls asleep, naked and white, trembling in the middle.

SIXTY
IN A GLASS

You tried to understand and I wanted to explain. You thought it would be easier with a dictionary in your hand. C'mon, academics seem to think that surfing is a water sport that consists in keeping your balance on top of a special board that glides along the crests of waves, or that it's a dance style from the sixties. They say that nihilism is the denial of all religious, political and social origins and principles. Denial of all belief. You say nothing and I say, between taking a drag and a sip, if there are no origins, perhaps there's no end. And if I seem to be a total son of a bitch, it's partly because I am, but I also have a heart as big as a whale. In the end we did it, and what we did was a sham at an inn called the Mundial with a very neat appearance and the odor of excessive public institutional zeal for hygiene. The reception area creaked with wooden antiquity. There was an old switchboard at the back of the reception desk with rows of jacks, some plugs for connecting directly with the rooms and in another corner of the reception area, a public telephone cabin with heavy wood and glass doors. It looked like a good place for communication. You are the princess of the pea and I'm the purple-faced man who has confused life with a joke in bad taste. I was expecting to find the swollen belly of your wolf, dressed as your grandmother, and rescue you and, for good measure, slash him like a dog. You were looking for a central European prince but then we saw each other up close, in the morning. You had sleepy breath and I had just curled up beside you, still wearing sunglasses. I redo my life as often as I redo the sheets on your bed. I always redo it after it has been shattered into a thousand pieces. I've never had the clarity to foresee practically anything. That night you partially desired me. Your pussy is elegant and discreet, coquettish and parsimonious. Slow, methodical and irascible. That night you didn't want me so close, only as close as necessary. As dawn broke, you invited me to a course on normality, free and intensive, attendance mandatory. It wouldn't work. It never worked. I've registered for several, but they wouldn't let me ask questions and they wouldn't let me cheat on the finals. I smiled as you asked me about my health, tidiness, attitude, hobbies, goals and ideals. You called me skinny cat. You were worried because you said I would get bored with you. Well, let me decide who I want to get bored with. You also said that you were too normal, but what you were trying to say was that I was abnormal, without my realizing it right away. When I went to see you off at the station, it all seemed to be a general rehearsal. Your face moving away in the subway, walking along the platform, returning to its natural state and, with every step, you were more beautiful.

SIXTY-ONE
COURT OF THE MYRTLES

In the West it is also known as the Patio of the Pond. The Pond reflects the four walls, attempting to soften the traditional sensation of verticality. The water is the greatest treasure of the palace. The canals, for all appearances simple, mischievously play with the flow of the water, becoming narrower so the water will flow faster through the curves. The water always falls noiselessly, laminated, never ceasing to appear mirror-like. Both public and private life occur in the patios. Audiences and rest periods take place there. In the winter, the sun shines on the patios, but not during the summer. The wind and water maintain a certain coolness in the area, which is also distributed by the blinds ....
Niches with perfumed water for the Sultan to wash with ...... The Hall of the Boat, no, ladies and gentlemen, there is no beached boat there, it is given that name because the interior, on the walls, the word Baraka appears, which means blessing, I think it is written .... in Kufic ....
.... as you might understand, this place contains as many treasures as information for explaining them. Of course, this wouldn't be the case if you'd chosen the guided tour with headphones. You'd have much more precision about the information, although not so much about the art, isn't that so? ... Okay, where were we? The Hall of the Boat was another of the areas exclusively for the Sultan. Here, there are many poems dedicated to water and written in the niches... I'll recite a couple for you. Let's see if I can remember them exactly... Here's the first one, "I am like the platform of a bride endowed with beauty and perfection" ... Ah, this, this one is also very good... "Gaze upon the urn and you will understand the truth of my words..." And now, of course, we pass to the Court of the Lions. No, don't be afraid, there aren't any living beasts, ha, ha... The name comes from a Jewish

vizier who ordered the bringing of twelve lion sculptures meant to represent the Twelve Tribes. The water that runs in and out is still the same water. Oh, here is another poem inscribed on the marble, "The water is like the tears of a lover striving to flow…" As you can see, the columns of this courtyard are distributed in a random manner, although they follow a sequence of three, one, one, two, one, two, two, one, two… And, finally, the Hall of the Abencerrajes, whose name comes from the fact that here they slit the throats of each and every one of the Abencerrajes. If you look where I'm pointing you can see the rust stains. Popular lore attributes this deterioration to the blood that was spilled here.

It was hot, the tourists perspired more than they listened. The guide, about to finish his shift, could only think about wetting his whistle with some gazpacho. I couldn't stop thinking about you, there, from here. I had already taken too many kisses from the jar, now that you were more and more convinced that I was an errant man. That I erred too much. That I was the erroneous guy.

SIXTY-TWO
WORK?

Chicho is talking about Deleuze and Burroughs, while having his first smoke of the morning. I woke up at La Quemada and brought Chicho breakfast. He asks me where I've been keeping myself all this time, putting the fruit and beer in the porta-fridge. Then he starts talking about capitalism and overproduction.

Chicho is frail, his skin is like an old suitcase. He doesn't have a television, he gets his electricity by tapping into a cable on a pole a few meters from his house, and he has a telescope. He grows lettuce, onions, beets, potatoes, peppers, pot and he raises chickens. I've never seen him wearing long pants or shoes. He has a thirteen-year-old daughter in Germany who he goes to see from time to time. He has a picture of her, neat and pretty, posing beside a dragon tree. A thousand books line the walls of his hut, pressed up against the stickers, disordered in stacks and piles. He has cataracts in one eye. He has the indeterminate age of tattoo-covered marines. Chicho would set off bombs, if he really wanted to. He talks about the disastrous twentieth century, which according to him will never end, as he prepares stewed coffee and warns me that I can't leave without having breakfast. The sea recently brought him an empty, broken and bloodstained raft. It's only good for firewood, so he's letting it dry outside the door. Passing taxis honk because it partially blocks the road. Chicho vents. "What do they expect me to do, take the oars out and park it better? The next one that says something I'm going to shut their trap."

Chicho likes the word, entropy. Entropy is life and life is shit, he says. According to the laws of physics, all systems decline into chaos, which is called entropy. The wearing out of an engine is entropy. A cut is entropy, a senseless mistake is entropy.

A needle in a haystack. A shift in tone or a volcanic eruption in a desolate crater. Time is the direction in which entropy moves. A cruel tendency on the part of the universe and all the systems it contains. All is careening towards a state of increasing disorder. He fries eggs on the grill. The black sand that builds up under his fingernails mixes with the pepper he uses to season them. He goes on to say that we have the dubious honor of bearing witness to a profound mutation of capitalism, rendering it even more omnivorous. Chicho is disillusioned with sabotage, group meetings and destructotherapy. He prefers the isolation of being on his Island. With a full stomach, we look out to a sea that never seems to get bored. Then he takes me into the hutch and, in a corner, where he's installed a skylight, he shows me a table over which presides a majestic laptop. He tells me you have to know your enemy. Chicho might be hanging back, but he's not an idiot. He turns it on and connects to the internet. He looks at the forecasts for the next few days, smearing the keys with egg yolk and suggests that if I want to enjoy the sea before the trade winds arrive, tomorrow afternoon there should be a bath worth taking. He shows me photographs of his daughter, organized in folders on his laptop and tells me he has always been discreetly unhappy, which is more than most people can say, and he curses globalization, laughing at his own new ability to connect to the world via an electrical network. He says, yes, the idea of mixing cultures is fine, converting the world, all the worlds, first, second and third, into one. But no one really believes in this.

"It's getting late, Chicho."

"Late, for what?"

"Well, for putting on my work shoes."

"Work? What a regression!"

In spite of everything, he lets me leave. He puts a Toots and the Maytals record on the turntable and rolls a fat one to smoke through the morning. Chicho knows I like listening to him, he switches from one subject to another and before I know it he's telling me my girlfriend is beautiful but he can't see us staying together. An egg and a chestnut won't last long together. I tell him we love each other and he laughs, asking me since when that's been enough. He says we look beautiful together, though we have our sights set differently. I don't say anything, I'm ready to leave. He turns the album over and starts talking about the waves. As he wipes up the crumbs from breakfast and takes them to the sink, he tells me that the composition of seawater is similar to that of blood plasma and that the body recovers equilibrium in the sea by osmotic absorption, and for that reason, without realizing it, he's tried to become an amphibian. He also tells me it contains eighty elements that are necessary for the proper functioning of the human organism, including anti-carcinogens, antibacterials and antivirals. I say goodbye and he tells me to come back whenever I want, that I don't have to bring him anything. Before putting my shoes on, in the van with the motor running, I pull out the jar of kisses. *Hurricane kisses. Skink kisses. High-tide kisses. Cloud vapor kisses. Silencer kisses. Kisses written with a finger on a misty mirror. Kisses face down on top of me. Revolutionary kisses. Gypsy kisses. Boiling kisses. Kisses offering you my boobs. Kisses back atcha. Pineapple kisses. S.O.S. kisses. Falling asleep kisses* I take one kiss out after another, gluttonous, without savoring them, gulping them, trying to drown myself.

Sixty-three
El Porís

As it happens, they always look for drowned people in the same place. The Island is perched in equilibrium on the verge of plummeting into an oceanic abyss. A sheer cliff, pitch black, perpetual. A short distance from the coast, The Island plunges hundreds of meters into submerged darkness where the creatures are monstrous scaled deformities. Their eyes are adapted to perceive infinitesimal quantities of light, or they don't have eyes at all. Stretched out on the beach while the sea is calm and the sun toasts my shoulders, it's hard to imagine what lies beneath. That's why I don't scuba dive. I returned to The Island, I always return. It was waiting for me. When someone mentions Crooknose, the words swirl in my mouth, but I'm left at a loss for how to respond.

"Maybe you'll run into him at the lighthouse in El Porís. In fact, the peak, the beach, the waves, the people, the sea and The Island, everything Crooknose said was his, is calmer now, happier."

The Island, thanks to its underwater abyss and the currents that cruise around it, has its own rules. Once they've floated past the barrier beach, the cadavers are spat out near the lighthouse at El Porís. The families of lost fisherman, the inhabitants of El Porís, even the authorities all know this fact. The laws of physics work like a drain hole. The day you find my board banging against the rocks, go look for me at El Porís.

SIXTY-FOUR
FLOATING TRASH

Feli was sitting in his van with the sliding door open. Not a wave on the sea. Through the window he could see the bay at The Sewer, transformed into a mere puddle. That day he had no girlfriend. He called me and said he needed to talk to someone. It seemed strange, his gestures always proclaimed self-sufficiency. He was reading a wave magazine with a giant breaker on the cover and ads inside. All in English, all done with photoshop, all for small change, including a free DVD.

I don't give a fuck about surfing. Surfing as leitmotiv or clothing in shop windows. Surfing in car advertisements, surfing as metaphor for investment funds or hair conditioners. Dawns spent in the water are priceless despite lost sleep. Despite the cold. The release of all those hormones, tautening your smiles. Another ancestral challenge, albeit drenching. It's not so different from cleaning your teeth with a toothpick in a bar, or masturbating when you can't get to sleep. It's pleasurable and it can become indispensable. So what if it rains while you wait for some waves in the water? When you get in the water, when the viscous light barely outlines the contours of the bay, you let out a scream as if you were dreaming, against a wall of water, frothing and effervescent, that's what interests me. That your mouth waters when you see it's snowing. That you can't sleep despite your exhaustion because when you close your eyes, the mind and body snake around again to some corner of the world in silence. That your wetsuit, almost dry, smells of firewood in the morning, having stared at the embers in the fireplace all night. That interests me. Before saying hello to him I watched him for a moment. I'm not sure if Feli had an erection or not, although he was impeccable as always. Ironing stains were visible on his Bermuda shorts. We've been abducted, American-style. The global colonization spreads like a black tide that is increasingly imperceptible. Globetrotters, libertines, freeloaders and adventurers. Extreme lives, bohemianism of the new era, all sponsored by some isotonic solution that gradually reduces the percentage of water in its composition. If you're young and rebellious, Papa Cash understands you. We go on dreaming we're special, and now you can buy clothing for special people from a catalogue. There are hell's angels with little hearts and intrepid archeologists who trust their deodorant. They go back to acquiring, it's not hard anymore, we're disposed to believe everything. Not the way of life, or the self-made man, or redefining the forbidden. Everything is now available on the kids level, where they'll always let you acquire your favorite fiction with a credit card and easy payment plan. Collecting expensive penchants and attractive toys, with accelerated depreciation. Everything has become inoffensive. We look like creations of the creative department. We are merely targets. We are made to learn English as we liberate endorphins. In its favor, English is succinct and onomatopoeic, as well as being the ultimate language. With English, we've learned to name, homogenously, diverse concepts, some quite terrible. Prow, fin, lasting freedom, improper behavior, or one hundred percent beef. They gave us the shaft a long time ago, they switched our Serrano ham for all-bran, and nobody seems to care. Feli was sad, he didn't have any new clothes, he was lonesome, he said he'd been playing playstation for days, and to top it off there weren't any waves, that if he could, he'd go live inside the DVD.

"Junk is the ideal product. The junk merchant doesn't sell his product to the consumer, he sells the consumer to his product."
William S. Burroughs, *Naked Lunch*

SIXTY-FIVE
IN THE BATHTUB

It's finally springtime for department stores, the television at the bar screams at me. I'm going to look for you. I need a fix of chocolate covered skin smelling of salt. *Kisses with the tongue. Butterfly kisses. Lower-my-straps kisses. Take-me-from-behind kisses. Sideways kisses. Metallic kisses. Turbulent space kisses. Tied to the bed kisses. Melancholic kisses. Urgent kisses. Tongue and nose kisses from the tips of your toes to the last hair on your head. Kisses on your bulges. Run-with-me kisses.* I digest them with my gut dancing on its axis of rotation. *Juicy playful kisses. Kisses spread on good morning toast. Kisses for no reason. Greasy kisses. Kisses on your eyes and hands. Watching a movie kisses. Coconut kisses. Kisses from exile. Take off my clothes and do it to me now kisses.* I would call you and try to translate the flutter in my stomach into something pronounceable so you could feel my pleasure, and I'd read all these kisses to you without stopping. *Profound kisses. Kisses all over your body. Kisses and licks. Toxic kisses. Bubbly kisses. Hot kisses.* You've probably gone out with your umbrella to look for Nico, the gecko, or a prince in blue shirt and white collar, or you go on restlessly staring at eggs and chestnuts trying to find their seven similarities. I still have two more kisses to open. One of the two is tied with a small piece of mauve twine, like the first one. You already told me not to expect too much from it. The penultimate one is a *Bathtub kiss*, with hot water and sponge in my hand. I'm going to pick you up so you can give me the last one in the jar. You're far away, but if I go, it's because you've grown even more silent.

Sixty-six
Melted Ice

The blue of Eric's eyes stuttered due to the smoke. Mostly, he stuttered because of the rat poison. He'd been self-medicating, conscientiously, for the last few hours. He was leaning on the bar, trying to get some service. It wasn't that they hadn't noticed him, of that he was sure. By bumping into the waitress, he'd made her drop a tray full of glasses and melted ice. Everyone at the bar turned, shaking their heads at the scene of this shabbily-dressed old guy misbehaving. They took their time serving him his second to last drink. The Big Kahuna is one of those bars for which all hope is lost that anything will ever happen. It is brightly lit and never empty. Until a few months ago it was called The Fuzzy Mermaid, it had more scum, less people and a bit of danger. I preferred it before. Now it's a beer pub with a modern look where you can drink corona and sometimes get sprayed by bubble-bath partiers. Of course, it's decorated with enormous photographs of surf legends: Pat Curren, Joel Tudor, Eddie Aikau, of course, Duke Pahoa Kahino Mokoe Hulikohola Kahana Moku, and Greg Nolan. Together with the photos there are foam board cutouts imitating enormous old boards from the early days. Ten flat-screen TVs feature ten different surfing videos on all five continents, so that furious solitary drinkers can have a drink without having to interact with anyone except the plasma. I said hello to Eric and, as soon as he recognized me, he offered me some poison. He was coming out of the bathroom, taking a sip, starting to talk. When he was under the influence, his French accent dissipated and he would go from glee to fear in the articulation of a monosyllable. I ordered rum and looked around at the women. They were all tanned and wearing loud Bermuda shorts, many were bleached blonds, with lots of illicit cleavage. They looked like bit players in the videos, but I'd never seen any of them in the water, not even on the beach. When I turned back to Eric, he was speaking inconsolably about his friend. Everyone supposed it must have been a huge wave, or another shark attack in the afternoon. Nobody'd heard from him in weeks. Eric couldn't stop worrying, his mood changed with every sip. His friend, well, his acquaintance, was kind of a tough guy, a video game thug, a real son-of-a-bitch, a role model for many, a solid buddy. His close friends quietly called him Silver Back, the alpha male gorilla of the troop. Eric admired the macho man, he referred to him as the boss monkey, a bit quarrelsome, whose nose he split in two a few years ago when things like that still happened outside the door of this bar. His description was of an impeccable match for my Crooknose. He who was always either on the beach or causing trouble somewhere. The last time Eric saw him, he was getting into the car with The Blonds, with their boards and gear. The last time I saw him, he was tied with his own leash to the car that crashed at The Sewer, begging for I don't know what. The sculpture to inner peace created by the woman with the beer can, shawl and child on the beach, had provided ammunition for his stoning. At no time did the tower of silence come tumbling down. Crooknose, yes. In the darkness and taken by surprise, he didn't recognize me, which was normal. A Silver Back only takes notice of other Silver Backs. That's how alpha males are. Eric accumulated bits of white saliva at the corners of his mouth as he spoke. He said he saw him surfing a lava break at La Machacona. Wow. He also said he'd been in jail for splitting some guy's face just to mark his territory like a dog peeing on curbs. Ha! That despite beating his women, women still loved him. Stupendous. That the Germans who settled here more than thirty years ago, those strange millionaires, viewed him with great respect. How wonderful. I told Eric it was me, that they could find him in the tangle of metal at The Sewer. Although, at this point, if he hasn't washed up at the lighthouse of El Porís, he'd probably been eaten by barracudas.

"The what?"

"The *bicudas*." Sometimes the simultaneous translation is difficult. Eric only spoke island dialect.

His eyes and mouth opened wide and he laughed out loud as he pounded me on the back and grabbed me by the arm.

"You're a stinking *godo*!" He tried to drag me to the bathroom again to share a snort of poison, pushing through the people, laughing uncontrollably, his glasses fogging up. I finished my rum, paid for the drinks, and went home. When I was saying goodbye, Eric opened the way for me by shoving his way to the back of the bar, to the back and to the right.

SIXTY-SEVEN
EL SOCORRO

The hooded figures wandered all over the beach. It wasn't the first time. The fishermen accompanied them in their mourning, though without much movement. They smoked and the smoke was bitter. Vapors rose from some of the parked vans and the fog saddened everything for as far as one could see. The wave died twenty months ago. The knife in the back could be seen in the middle of the sea and they called it the breakwater. The exodus of shoals of fish only served to confirm the tragedy, dogs spun nervously, leaving swirled tracks in the sand. Eric would come along with his son to pick up trash, rubbing salt in the wound. He was one of those inhabitants of The Island who, although he was sick of it, was trapped there forever. "I sheet on zee Macaronesia, zee Fortunate Islands, zee juice bars, zee cheese deep, zee seezoned meat chunks, and zee customs." His son laughed with delight because his father was crazy and he liked that, perhaps that's why he was bald and spoke with a French accent, perhaps that's why he wore thick-lensed glasses. "I sheet on zee fight r-r-rings, zee insularitay, zee beech sheet and zee *leche y leche*." Eric still couldn't understand how some people could claim The Island, the beach, the waves as their own at the same time as they covered it all over with their shit. The conceited town, not entirely neglected, had lost the colorfulness, often color-blind, of towels, boards, wetsuits and midday snacks on the terrace when it isn't raining. Their brows knit and their boards once more in their cases. The mist dispersed when someone pointed toward the horizon. A gentle rise and fall disrupted the sea's plate-like routine. The next day the timidity gave way to small ripples that angled towards the cement prosthesis with the intention of washing it away over time. A few months later, the days began rambunctiously. Cars pulled up happily with the music blaring. Jests and mist. Fishermen fixing their nets and many smiling onlookers. Chicho no longer goes to El Socorro, nor does he go to the cemetery on the eve of all saint's day, but that doesn't mean he isn't thinking of his father. He maintains a suffering and surly silence in this respect. When you mention the breakwater, he stands up, clenches his jaws, stares into your eyes blaming you for everything, and leaves.

After the summer, there are those who still prefer to get in the water out there, to the left and nowhere else. That's love. The force of nature is superimposed on this anthropomorphic cancer, even though no rehabilitation ever completely ends. Little by little, the days you can never forget return with the breakers—El Socorro brings in really good waves—they're celebrated with bonfires at night and the aroma of grilled sardines. The sailors smile with their taut brows as the enthusiastic villagers are once again covered with colors.

Sixty-eight
Rough Weather

A warm wind emerges from the depths of the soil, from where one can no longer distinguish what is the earth and what is not. Hot wind. Night is falling. There are still people who haven't reached their homes and practice the dance of frightened ants in the street. Oblique, violent rain. The trees, who know us, split in front of us and die in the road. The high-voltage electrical towers forever bow down before the brute force roaring from the cliffs. The idiotic grandeur of the industrial plants, pure rubbish. The villages don't make a sound. Perhaps there is nothing left outside. Here, inside, the electrocardiogram of a candle is cast into a corner. We assess the damages, glued to a radio. Try to get some sleep. Stay in your homes. Buy or loot if the supermarket is still standing. Don't leave your transistor radios. Don't go to work unless absolutely necessary. Follow directions precisely and no one will get hurt. Lightning splitting speed limit signs. Groundswells punishing the piers.

I decided to go out and take a look at the sea, to thrill to the fear of its ferocity. The village, the entire coast, the bay, until then so pleasant, was now beaten down by the maritime fury. The marbled, churning sea, like the locks of a frightened child. I smoked in the shelter of the van's interior. That was enough for the clouds, who were lurking just beyond the horizon, to pounce upon me, treacherously attacking me with their incontinence. Before I realized it, the rain had delighted in pouring in through the window. I sat there for a while doing nothing, then for three days after that I was mopping up water. The rain subsided and I went down to the beach. It was delirious, completely crazed.

Two days later I came again and it was abating, transitory mental disorder. I had my board with me to check it out.

Entrusting myself to the water and overcoming the first wall of foam was an absolute act of faith. It was too much, it was huge, it sounded massive. A vast sea, churning and ferocious, yet disposed to grant a few good lashes, some static sparks from a friend you haven't seen in a long time. When I came out of the water, the sun was low, and I didn't see it. The wrecked car, which for months had presided over the beach, near the rocks, was there no longer. The car we'd watched rusting, where I had tied Crooknose, was gone. During that gale no one could have come to The Sewer with a crane to remove it. The sea had swallowed it on one of those days when there wouldn't have been anyone to witness and accuse it. With a single strike, a powerful tongue and a piece of candy, there wouldn't have been any resistance. Walking along the beach, I found the engine block completely torn loose, and a little further on, the leash, desperately gnawed at by Crooknose, tossed upon the wet sand, which the sea would soon wash away. No one seems to know where the car ended up. One sunny day, on a transparent and glassy sea, we'll find it under the crest of a wave. We'll play around above it, like a shoal of hungry fish.

SIXTY-NINE
DRY

I don't remember it very clearly, but the other day I went around a couple of turns, trusting in the frivolity with which they'd been conceived. It must have happened during one of them. After the impact, I spent several hours wandering through the waiting rooms taking care of the last ghostly procedures. My purgatory, like other devices for paying attention to what lies beyond, mine was personalized with all kinds of details, but the roaming was also painful. A journey that always seemed endless. I drove, I don't remember, fifty, sixty hours on side roads, with the sun in my eyes at all times, reflecting off the windshield, I could hardly guess at where the road lay. I only stopped twice to eat something and stretch my legs. My feet hurt. Part of my penitence included some terrible orthopedic shoes, custom-made, but not for me. Work shoes: new, stiff and polished, which could be worn on either foot because they always felt like they had the form of the other. They squeezed my toes and arches, preventing me from thinking clearly. There was no way to take them off, they forced me into humiliating positions. I was traveling with your jar, of course. The jar was still transparent, but now it was slippery. A fine film of your fluids made it impossible to grab. I tried to put it with my gear, but it kept slipping out. The rest of the trip would involve juggling, trying to keep the jar from shattering. The bar at the side of the highway was infested with dry, rancid and sour beings. A village on a plateau, without sea or mountain. One of the walls of the bar was simply fuel for the flames, but nobody seemed to care. I did. My ice melted, and anything plastic fused with the stinking bar. Before the customers could cover their drinks, protecting them from the debris, I saw a smiling gecko, stuck to the wall, as his skin shriveled up, twisting in the inferno. Suddenly everything went dark. I stopped the van and looked for a bed. I found an empty one together with seven occupied beds in a room without windows. The sleepers writhed in their sheets, stained with blood. They smelled of garlands of dried flowers, submerged in mud. In no time, German nurses from WWII appeared, their bleached blond hair was black at the roots. They kicked the door down and threw my companions onto stretchers like sacks of potatoes. I had dinner, accompanied by the jar, which spent most of the time in the air, as I wildly danced around trying to keep it from falling to the floor, first with one hand, then the other. I got up early, strapped the jar into the passenger's seat with a seat belt and drove the van to a port, struggling to keep the jar from falling. It kept sliding all over the place. I drove off in the van certain that the ship would sink as soon as the road toward the horizon tired of shrinking. That's exactly what happened. I arrived at the train station, waited an hour and a half and, as I was waiting, avoided, out of fear, the armed commandos with open umbrellas who viciously attacked, disfigured and splattered the guts of anyone who didn't have one of those devices in hand. It's difficult to escape from almost certain death while you're worrying about your jar breaking and scattering its paltry contents. I traveled another six hours. I got off at another station and waited two and a quarter hours. I took another train, for five more hours. I reached the environs of an airport. Another three and a half hours staring at a fish tank with a grouper that copulated with every single one of the other species in his company. He went after the pale jellyfish with a voracity that sent water overflowing the aquarium, splashing the waiting room with a cold noise that was curiously dry. I waited another interminable two hours and then glanced at the Notebook that had been hidden at the bottom of my backpack for such a long time. Hardly anything more would fit on its filthy, swollen pages. In purgatory some faces were more tired than mine. I boarded a plane and got off three and a half hours later. I caught a ride that took me to an intermediate point, and thus lost and remote from any highway on The Island. I waited one hundred seventy-four minutes for you to come and get me, and then just when I was getting good at keeping the jar in my hands for short periods, since it was still covered with your oils, it fell to the ground. I ran after it as it calmly rolled along, downhill, crossing all three lanes of the highway. I caught it, intact and sealed. One solitary kiss remained inside, the last, folded and tied with a mauve thread, desperately flapping, banging against the walls of the glass jar.

It must have been a car accident, or an air disaster, perhaps someone shot me in the head. In any case, my passage through purgatory was tedious but bearable. Surprisingly, it came to an end. And then, for no apparent reason, assuming that our final destination is Avernus, a bureaucratic error, or some other fluke, in the end, I was saved. The key to Paradise was hanging from your neck when you appeared like an angel wearing pajamas under your coat and eyes swollen from sleep. When I kissed you, you smelled of your house, but there was no trace of metal. A blend of earth, grapefruit and an exquisite suggestion of your infinity hidden within your clothing. We arrived at your house and embraced again, in contact with something that had evaded us for too long. I went out to get my bags from the car and then the front of your house was blue like the flame of a butane lighter, even trembling in the same way. The jar was dry, although it was so dirty that it seemed translucent. Faint candlelight on the stairs promised more above, in the bedroom. I touched you, urgently, perhaps my hands were all that certified my own demise. You invited me up to the room, to relax for a while, alone. A wonderful gesture that I accepted, frightened. I carefully went up the creaking stairs to the bedroom. It was all so clean and organized, I observed, trying to find some terrible new feature added to the room. Gradually, I was convinced that everything was in its place. Four candles on little tables, each with a puddle of wax flowing over your books. The closed window with its crystal curtain, static, abundant, with soothing colors. I glanced toward the bathroom. The flickering candles on the floor showed me the way. I moved slowly, causing the wooden floorboards to creak yet again. A large yellow cylindrical candle rested on the ledge of the bathtub and the tub was full. Full of water, bubbles and freshness. White rose petals floating on the steaming surface of the water and foam like fresh whipped egg whites. I felt it with my hand and it was scorching, but also oily. It was redolent of mandarin orange bath salts. Three stems of lavender were scuba diving beneath the foam, as well as a grapefruit peel, complete and all in one piece. In no time I undressed and gently slid into the boiling tub. Once my temperature was equal to the water's, I submerged almost my entire body, excluding only my feet, nose and mouth. My body was still and without a pulse. I played with the petals, put my head underwater, soaked for long enough to wrinkle my fingers and turn my lips purple. I couldn't help wondering if there would be good waves in the morning. Immediately, I recalled the sound of dawn at The Sewer. My body deconstructed, it released, all the folds of the trip through purgatory extended. I enjoyed the expansion. Then you came up and asked how I was doing.

"Dead, and it's better than they say it is."

You kneeled beside the tub and kissed me slowly, the way only you can. You caressed me without caring about getting your sleeve wet. You stroked my chest and then my belly, very slowly. You took the big sponge, soaked it, and squeezed the scalding water it held over my legs, my chest, my face. A sexless, slippery and gigantic god softly squirmed over me. You kissed me again and passed the sponge over my entire body. I was rubber. The sponge floated around me and you touched my sex underwater, caressing it in all different ways. It surfaced and you rocked it in your hand. You sucked my face and neck. The water had turned me to driftwood. Your hand went lower and you entertained yourself finding places that sent me into spasms. You found several. Then you put the tip in your mouth, holding it there, resting your squeezed lips just at the water's surface. You nibbled and sucked, staring into my eyes. For a moment, the thought of that last kiss sitting in the kitchen came to my mind, and what you'd said about it.

"Don't get your hopes up."

Later, in the morning, after you'd gone, I would go downstairs to make coffee. The kitchen would be meticulously clean and my nearly empty jar would sit in the center of the table. The last, folded piece of paper, with its knotted thread, would wait, inert, at the bottom of the jar. I would feel a coldness but pretend to ignore it by having a good breakfast. When it was no longer avoidable, I would open the jar and insert my hand. I would take out the scrap of paper and carefully untie the knot. Then I would take the kiss in my hand, gazing toward the cliffs outside the window. *No more kisses.* Tremendous cold.

You stopped before my heart leapt from my mouth and became confused with the sponge. You stood, splashing a bit of water, and left in silence, demolishing me with your green eyes. I dried off, unable to recognize my own body. After my bath I found you beneath the sheets. I lay down beside you and felt that you were naked. You lay on top of me. We unmade the bed. You screamed incredibly loud. So loud you shattered the crystal curtains. You sucked on my hand when I put my hand close to your mouth, to muffle you. You tore pieces of my flesh between your cries. I sucked your feet and your breast with so much fervor, wanting to swallow them, and you pushed me furiously away. You turned over. I grasped your hips, raising you upward. We were only able to stop when the snooping sun peeked in through the window. Our legs were trembling. Our mouths were empty. We slept, one on top of the other.

I don't remember who was on top of whom.

HUGO CLEMENTE (Salamanca, Spain. 1973)

With a degree as a social psychologist, Hugo Clemente has been teaching Spanish at several universities in Boston since 2015. He coordinated the Canarian School of Literary Creation (2013-2015), but also has worked as a therapist at a methadone program, a surf and snowboard instructor and as a Dj among others. He has been teaching Creative Writing Workshops in different Spanish cities as well as in New York, Boston and Stamsund (Norway).

He was finalist at *LuchaLibro* (First Literary Improvisation Championship held in Spain, 2012) and has also participated in other collections of stories: *PervertiDos* (Editorial Traspiés, Granada, 2014), *Ménades: an invitation to euphoria* (La Piscina Editorial-Keroxen, Tenerife, 2015) and has scripted for theater and cinema. His last documentary, *The Blinking Island* (2016), has been selected in the official section in different festivals (Miradas.Doc, Canarias Surf Film Festival, Madrid Surf Film Festival, Portugues Surf Film Festival, Bombay Water Film Festival, Surf & Music & Friends Festival...), nominated at Concepción Independent Film Awards (Chile) and awarded with Best Script at MIMPI Fest (Brazil) 2017 and the Audience Award at Mequinenza International Film Festival 2017 (Spain).

He has collaborated with various media such as the *International Journal of Iberian Studies*, *Mondo Sonoro*, *Los Bárbaros* (NY), *Calviva*, *Píldora Sonora*, and regularly publishes in his blog ¡No toques nada! He also works in translation and literary proofreading.

Cuaderno de Agua (Novela. Canalla Ediciones, Madrid, 2012), which is about to exhaust its third edition, was translated by Peter Khan as *Water Log* during 2016.

Lightning Source UK Ltd.
Milton Keynes UK
UKHW03f1810020718
325121UK00001B/69/P